5 DAYS

A DEE SANDERS ADVENTURE

LP SNYDER

5 Days is a work of fiction. Any references to historical events, real people, or real places are used fictitiously. Other names, characters, places, and events are products of the author's imagination, and any resemblance to actual events or places or persons, living or dead, is entirely coincidental.

2025 Sky Blue Stories Paperback Edition

www.skybluestories.com

ISBN: 978-1-7355084-8-1

Cover art by Vince Conti and Elizabeth Mackey

Map by Jamie Lee Scott

This book is dedicated to Dr. David H. Sexton, world traveler and inspiration for this story.

PREFACE

When the night turned old and the stars looked down,
and you hugged yourself on the cold, cold ground,
you woke the morning in a stranger's coat,
no one would you see.
You'd ask yourself, who'd watch for me,
my only friend, who could it be?

—It's Probably Me-Gordon Sumner/Michael Kamen/Eric Clapton (Sting)

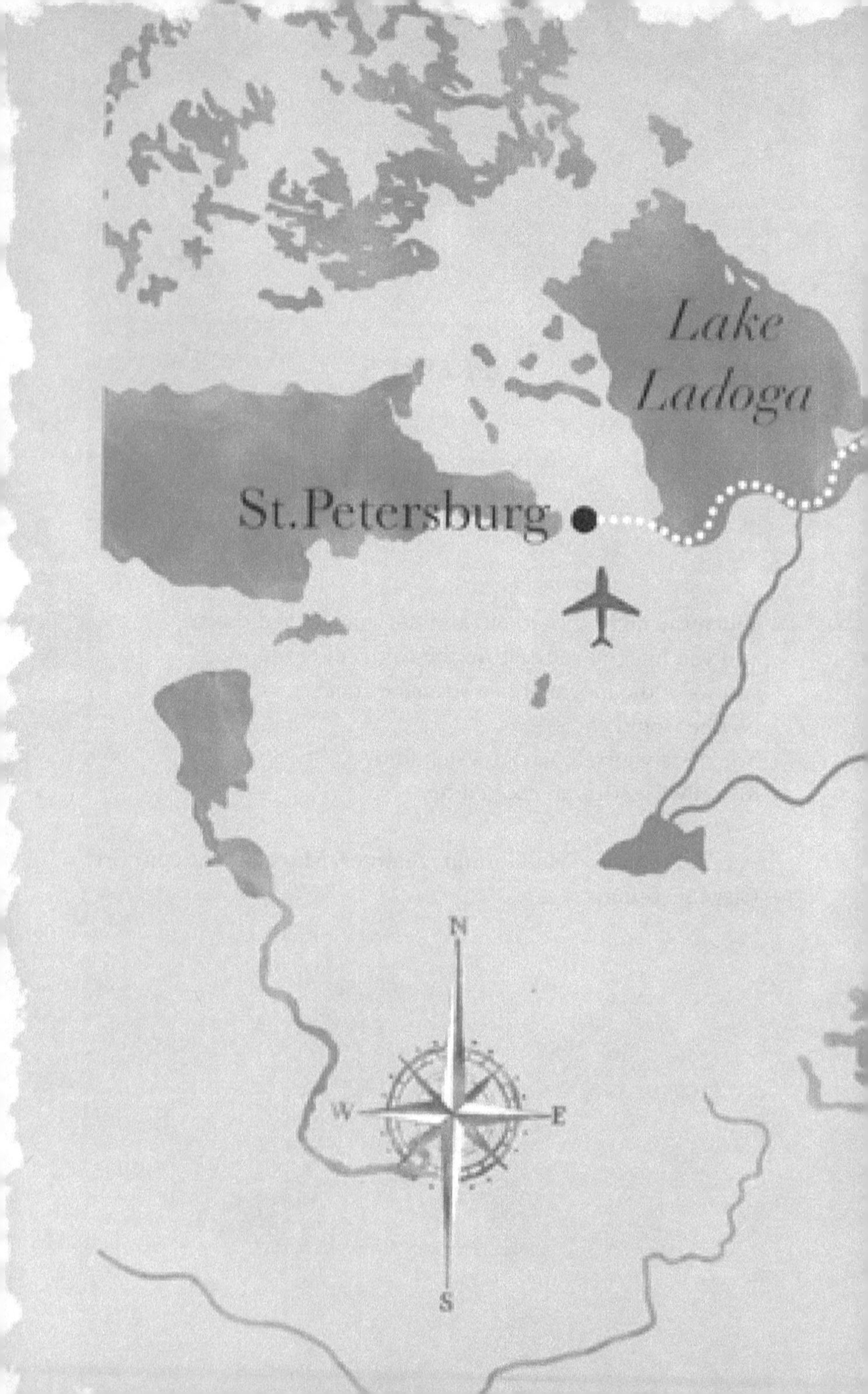

Lake Ladoga
St.Petersburg
N
W
E
S

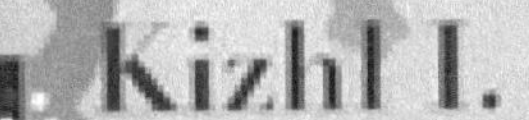

Kizhl I.
Svir River
Lake Onega
Volga-Baltic Waterway
Mandrogi
Goritsy
Rybinsk Reservoir
Uglich
Yaroslavl'
Volga River
Moscow

PROLOGUE

The sun is a white-hot light burning bright as thin cirrus clouds streak across a high blue sky, tree tops dancing in the wind. Yeah, that's how it feels.

I'm running for my life. I have been for most of the night, one step in front of the other. *One more step, breathe, one more step*, I keep telling myself. *Don't stop. They're coming.*

I look back at my dog, a spaniel named Jemmy. He is loping along behind me, his eyes bright and his tongue lolling. I take another stride. I have to get to the church. If I stop, he'll stop. Then they'll kill us both.

There is a pearl clutched in my hand. It is the size of an ostrich egg and had belonged to my mother. She'd told me to protect it. There was a place I could go, a man who could help me, if only I could get there.

I've been running for hours, my lungs heaving, heart in my throat, breathing ragged, feet blistered. I stumble in a gopher hole and nearly fall as I feel my ankle turn. Hobbling now, I keep on, knowing the place I seek grows closer.

But I can hear them coming, the galloping horses, the shouts of the men, the grind of machinery, drawing ever near.

I top a small knoll and can see the church in the distance, across a flat expanse of ground. Only a little farther to go, if I can just keep running. Getting closer I can see the graveyard and the markers, hard stone fingers reaching into the sky, beckoning me on.

Taking a quick glance over my shoulder, I can see the men on horseback coming over the knoll. I am halfway to the church and faltering fast. Then I see him. The pastor standing in the yard at the gate, an arm rose in salute. I speed up but I don't know how. Jemmy pulls up beside me, panting heavily but matching my stride. We are close.

I feel the ground tremble as the men on horseback grow nearer. I hear sounds and the dirt behind me springs up and attacks the backs of my legs. There is shouting.

The pastor stays in the yard, his face frozen as both the riders and I approach. Watching him, I see his mouth drop open and his eyes go blank.

I can't hear anything, but I feel my body rack in pain, a series of beats, like a hammer on tin, running across my shoulders.

There's a yelp, I heard it clearly. Glancing down, I see Jemmy is no longer striding beside me but rolling on the ground, thrashing, as if fighting with invisible snakes.

I stumble, only feet from the gate. Lunging forward, I roll the pearl toward the pastor, like a bowling ball headed for a pin.

His face momentarily comes to life, and I see him step over the pearl and conceal it with his robe.

I tumble to the ground, a mouth full of grass welcoming me.

It is July, 1918, and my name is Anastasia Romanoff.

PROLOGUE TWO

Nine Months Earlier

It is cold. Winter comes early here. We arrived just before dawn. The sky is swirling above us, around us, and the wind howls as if in pain. It has not been easy, but there is much at stake.

I am dressed in a heavy, long, brown woolen coat and a cap that matches. There is a red band wrapped around the outside of my upper arm. It circles the area of my biceps. I have heavy, mud-crusted boots upon my feet. The long walk across the fields to get here was slippery and hazardous. My face, wrinkled and dirty from the journey, is heavily bearded to protect against the cold. I am not an old man, but I feel like one.

In my left hand, clutched by near frozen fingers, is a Mosin-Nagant model 1891 rifle with a sixteen-inch bayonet. I've had to use it today and will probably do so again. It was not without purpose.

I was left alone by the others to guard this entrance. As the wind picks up, daylight feels like a long way away. I shiver and feel the cold sting upon my cheeks. Pushing the door open I stumble inside. There is time before the others return.

Walking down a short hall, I turn and enter a grand room. It is enormous. Everything is red and gold wherever I turn. Then I see it, across the way. Sitting on a platform six steps high is a red velvet and gold chair. Behind it on the wall is the winged golden crest of Imperial Russia. I am in the Throne Room of the Winter Palace. It is empty and I stand there alone. I gaze upward at the inlaid ceiling, then down to the marbled floor. Never before have I seen anything like it.

I climb the steps slowly and approach the throne. The end of each golden arm is shaped like a lion's head. On one side there is a pearl the size of an ostrich egg. I turn my gaze to the other arm, expecting to see a mate, but instead, only a space where another pearl has been. Who took it? I should leave, lest I be accused. As my gaze turns upward to the Imperial crest, I see a jeweled dagger embedded in a sheath. It has a handle of gold, studded with gems. Pulling the dagger from its place in the crest, it has a stunningly sharp steel blade. Whatever the risk, I hurriedly hide it in my overcoat. As I turn and stare, there is a gleam in my eyes. Despite the worn and weathered face, it shines nearly as bright as the gold of the throne.

Climbing down the steps I see the mud from my boots smeared across the marble floor. There is nothing I can do but return to the outside, to my post. The room begins to lighten and I look toward the window, the beams spilling inside and hovering in the air, like butterflies on the breeze, between the massive ivory columns that support the ceiling.

I have never seen such decadence. There are sounds, and more of the soldiers of my brigade rush into the room. I step in front of the throne to hide the missing pearl and shift uncomfortably from foot to foot. The Czar and his family were taken away from here. I hope that does not happen to me.

It is October, 1917, and my name is Sergei Dimitrov.

1

____

DEE & FRIENDS - TRAVELOGUE

Present Day

We left Amsterdam after a few weeks; got that itchy feeling again, time for something new. But we liked the house on the canal in Amsterdam and decided to keep it.

It was a short cruise from the North Sea to the Baltic Sea. Leaving Amsterdam at night, we were in Oslo in a day and a half. With a short stop there, we were then on to Copenhagen, Stockholm, Helsinki, and then terminated in St Petersburg, Russia. What next?

We signed up for a five-day river cruise on a longship that would take us from St. Petersburg to Moscow, with stops in between. We had two days in St. Petersburg and then would depart in the late afternoon of the third day.

Sitting on the balcony of mine and Gina's room at the Lotte Hotel, we were overlooking the Moyka River as the sun set and the lights of St. Petersburg came up.

"What does everyone want to do while we're waiting?" asked Dee.

"What is there to do?" asked Keno.

"Tour the city," replied Angelic. Keno gave her a sour look.

"Sit here in the hotel or go shopping?" asked Gina.

"What's the river cruise going to be like this time?" asked Mike.

"Aren't the Hermitage Museum and the Winter Palace here?" said Jamal.

"Yeah, they are nearby. No more than a few minutes away, along the Neva River," replied Dee.

"No," said Keno and Gina simultaneously.

"It's the second largest art museum in the world. It's full of amazing things—jewelry, gold, tapestries, sculptures, paintings, plus the building itself was left over from the czars. It's beyond decadent," replied Jamal.

"How do you know all this?" asked Angelic.

"Diego was telling me about it when we were working in Spain. He said to be sure and see it if we were anywhere close."

"It's so large that the half-day tour is nothing but a fast walk with no stops," said Dee.

"That sounds about right," answered Keno.

"Look we'll make a deal," said Dee. "We'll do the museum tomorrow, all day, so we can actually see something. The next day we'll shop or whatever you ladies want to do."

"Why can't we shop while you guys go look at the museum?" asked Gina.

Angelic nodded in agreement.

"I think it's safer if we all stay together. It's a big city. We don't know anything about it and we don't speak the language," said Dee.

"Dee's right. We need to stay together. I guarantee you'll see some things you like," added Jamal.

"And if we don't?" asked Angelic.

"The shopping is on me."

"It was always on you," replied Angelic.

Mike grinned and then spoke, "I heard you say it. Shopping is on you."

Dee looked at Jamal and then the rest of the group. "The GUM store here isn't likely to have much of anything you want."

"I think you're wrong about that," replied Angelic. "I looked it up. Shopping could be expensive."

Jamal sat back in his chair and sighed, to the laughter of the others.

———

BRIGHT AND EARLY THE NEXT MORNING THEY TOOK A TAXI TO the Hermitage Museum, which was only a few blocks across the river. It dropped them at the entrance, and they joined the already long line of tourists waiting for admission.

"We may spend all day waiting," said Keno.

"Or once we get inside, we may never want to leave," replied Jamal.

"You're dreaming buddy," said Mike.

Gina smiled at Dee and squeezed his hand. "I'm sure it'll be fun." Scanning the building with her other hand shielding her eyes, she added, "It's enormous."

"Part of the structure is the Winter Palace and part of it is the Hermitage Museum," replied Dee.

"Built all at once?" asked Mike.

"Over time and with various additions. Empress Elizabeth started it in the 1750s and Catherine the Great finished it over the course of her reign. There are five buildings, with the largest being the Winter Palace. It has over a thousand rooms. It was the official residence of the czars from the 1760s until the revolution," replied Dee.

"How do you know this stuff?" asked Keno.

"I read a lot."

————

THE LINE TRUDGED ALONG SLOWLY AS THEY MADE THEIR WAY TO the Palace Gate, into the courtyard beyond, and to the vestibule where they were admitted. They had arrived an hour prior to opening, and it had taken that long to reach the entrance. As they moved closer, the ornate nature of the palace became more apparent. The wrought iron gate capped by the double-headed eagle, symbol of Imperial Russia, was flanked by ornate gold-topped Corinthian columns. They were stepping into a different world and a different time.

Entering the palace, they approached the main staircase, surrounded by gold and gilt, with murals floating overhead on the ceilings. It was the most ornate structure any of them had ever seen.

"Where do we start?" asked Keno.

"At the beginning," replied Dee.

"Wiseass," she replied.

"Seriously, this is the main staircase. We join one of the guided groups, and they lead us through on the day tour."

"No way are we getting through this in a day," said Gina.

"We couldn't get through it in a week," added Mike.

"Let's just see what we can," replied Jamal.

They moved forward toward a short, dark-skinned woman holding a paddle that said, "Group 8."

She nodded and spoke. "Welcome to the State Hermitage Museum and Winter Palace. We'll begin shortly, as soon as we gather a few more visitors."

Milling about the staircase, they watched throngs of people scurrying past, speaking a wide range of languages, apparently from all over the world.

Jamal leaned in close to Dee and whispered, "This should be good."

The guide waved the group forward, and they ascended the two-tiered Jordan Staircase. It was like being inside a fairy tale, all white and gold, ornate and intricate, with marble statutes of many of the Greek gods.

"This is unbelievable," said Keno.

"Told you that you'd like it," replied Jamal.

"We will be turning to the left at the top of the stairs," called out the guide. "We will be entering the Field Marshals' Room."

"Wow," said Jamal. "Look at the size of the oil paintings."

"Look at the size of the room," added Keno.

"Who are these dudes?" asked Mike.

"Anyone that was ever honored as a Field Marshal in the Russian empire. Considered to be their greatest military leaders," replied Dee.

"Look at the chandeliers," said Angelic.

"Do you suppose they held dances in here?" asked Gina. "This would make a great ballroom."

"Probably too formal for even a ball. They have 999 other rooms. I bet several of them are designated as ballrooms," replied Dee.

"We'll be moving along to the Small Throne Room now," said the guide. They followed along behind, continuing to move left through the building.

It was a small room in comparison to the hall they'd just been inside, but still, it was grand in every way.

The guide stopped in front of a small alcove with a raised platform.

"This is the Small Throne Room of Peter the Great. You will notice the walls are lined with crimson velvet, decorated with the double-headed eagle of Imperial Russia sewn in silver thread. The gold-crested small domed arch above the throne is supported by two jade columns. The throne is said to be made of ivory coated in pure gold. You will note the lion heads at the end of each arm of the throne. The indented circular space on the top of each head was for two large pearl orbs, or eggs. One of them is on display further along the tour. It was secured for its safety, given pearls of that size are very rare. The other pearl disappeared during the revolution in 1917 and has never been recovered."

"Were the pearl eggs Fabergé?" Gina asked Dee, who was standing beside her.

"I don't know," replied Dee.

"You're supposed to know that stuff," whispered Keno, who was standing on Dee's other side.

Gina waved her hand at the guide, who stopped speaking. "Were the pearl eggs Fabergé?"

"Of course. Nicholas II had them made for his wife Alexandra, who then insisted he display them on the arms of the throne."

Jamal had approached Dee and whispered, "Fascinating." He slipped as he turned back toward Angelic, but Dee caught him by the shoulder.

"I told you not to wear those leather-soled shoes to the palace. You know the floors are marble and slick," said Angelic. The guide looked toward her.

"Sorry, just setting my husband straight."

The guide smiled. "Someone has to do it." She pointed toward the door. "We'll be moving on toward the Great Throne Room, or St. George's Hall."

"What was the purpose in having two throne rooms?" asked Jamal.

"The Great Throne Room was for formal, large functions, state events. The Small Throne Room was for more intimate settings, one-on-one visits with dignitaries, or family events. Nicholas felt safer there. It's why he allowed Alexandra to place the pearl eggs on the arms of the throne," replied the guide. "We'll be moving to the Armorial Hall, which was the reception area for the Great Throne Room when there were formal engagements."

As they moved into the hall, it was another grand, ornate room of white and gold, balconied around its perimeters.

"Did the czars really live like this?" asked Keno.

"Apparently so," replied Angelic. "At least until they didn't."

Through a doorway in the middle of the room, they moved into the Gallery of 1812 or the Military Gallery.

The guide stopped. "This room is full of portraits of the military leaders of the Patriotic War of 1812, fought against Napoleon, where the Imperial Russian forces repelled the French."

It was a long narrow room with a high ceiling, lined completely with oil paintings. The guide paused and while the rest of the group lingered near the middle, Jamal and Dee slowly made their way toward one end of the hall, studying the portraits as they went.

Nearing the end of the hall, Jamal on one side and Dee on the other, they approached the massive portrait of Alexander I, the czar during the Patriotic War.

"I reached it first," called Jamal.

He turned quickly and spun, but Dee was too far away this time and Jamal went down hard. Angelic shouted, and her footsteps rang in the corridor as she went running toward them.

Standing beside Jamal, Dee asked, "Are you okay?"

He grinned up at Dee, his eyes glazed. "Brace yourself, here she comes."

Angelic reached them with the guide close behind.

"I told you about those shoes," she exclaimed as she bent to her knees and placed her hand upon his face. "Tell me what hurts."

"My head is throbbing a little and my ears are ringing." His eyes were blinking, and he seemed to be staring at the ceiling.

"Lie still and breathe," Angelic replied.

"Is he alright?" asked the guide.

"Let him lie here for a moment. Is there a wheelchair?"

A burly, broad-shouldered man in a navy blazer appeared pushing one. He stood nearby, scowling at them.

Jamal continued to stare at the ceiling. He motioned to Dee.

"The Armorial isn't as deep as the Great Hall."

Dee looked at him, his face blank. "Not as deep," he said.

"What's he saying?" asked Angelic.

"Not sure."

"Let's get him in the wheelchair," said the burly guard who had appeared at his side. "We need to move him."

He rolled Jamal to the entrance as the rest of the group tagged along behind. Mike waved down a couple of taxis and the guard moved Jamal toward the second one. He pointed to the first cab. "Most of you get in there. We'll load him back here." Gina, Keno, and Mike got in the first taxi.

The guard and Dee loaded Jamal into the second taxi. As Jamal leaned forward from the wheelchair, the guard spoke to Dee. "What did he say when he was on the floor?"

Dee shook his head. "He mumbled something, maybe about the painting or that he was turning. I couldn't make out what he said."

The guard looked at Dee harshly. "I heard him say something about the depth of the hall."

Dee shrugged his shoulders as he slid in behind Jamal. "I don't know. I didn't hear. I was surprised and confused."

The guard closed the door as another car pulled up

behind. As the taxi pulled away, Dee looked over his shoulder to see the guard climb in the vehicle.

I don't normally consider myself paranoid, thought Dee, *but after that business in Eastern Europe with Olga and Boris, my internal alarm is going off. Jamal was just a tourist who slipped in the hallway of a tourist attraction. What possible problem could that be? I've just watched too many B-grade spy movies or read too many cheesy espionage novels.*

2

DEE & FRIENDS - HOTEL HEADACHE

They transported Jamal to his room in a wheelchair Angelic obtained from the concierge. She and Dee propped him up on pillows against the headboard while Mike returned the chair to the lobby.

While the rest of the group sat around the bed talking, Angelic monitored Jamal's neurological skills for evidence of a concussion. She had him follow her finger with his eyes, asked him how many fingers she held up, what was his name, what floor of the hotel they were on.

Jamal played along, answering her questions and smiling at her until she finished.

"I really just have a headache and feel a little weak."

Mike came back into the room and sat down. "When I was turning in the wheelchair, I'd swear that I saw the guard, or the guy from the museum that brought their chair to us, sitting in the lobby. I was sideways to him but it sure looked like the same guy, blue jacket, short hair, big man."

"That's odd," Dee replied.

Jamal moaned slightly, and everyone jumped. Angelica checked his forehead for temperature and offered him some water. He took a small sip and said, "I think I want to rest now."

"Okay," she replied.

"If you need anything, let us know," said Dee as he, Gina, Mike, and Keno got up to leave. Angelic nodded.

As the group moved down the hall toward their own rooms, Gina spoke, "I guess we should stay close, maybe get some lunch in the restaurant downstairs?"

"I'll stretch my legs and go down to see what their hours are and maybe grab a menu," said Dee.

The others nodded as Dee walked to the elevator. It picked him up quickly, and he rode to the lobby. Getting out and walking toward the restaurant, he saw the man Mike had mentioned. It was the guy from the museum. There was another similar-looking man sitting across from him. Dee looked beyond them and there was another man near the lobby doors.

Three big burly guys in blue blazers, one of them specifically from the museum, sitting in our lobby after Jamal fell. Why could that possibly be?

When Dee got back to the room, Angelic and Gina were sitting in the two armchairs in the living room chatting.

Angelic turned and said, "Jamal wants to talk to you. He asked that I give you a minute. Any idea what that's about?"

Dee shook his head at her. "No, but I'll go find out and keep you posted."

She nodded and smiled. "Thank you."

"Maybe some guy thing?"

"I'm a nurse. I worked emergency room before I specialized. He knows that."

"Maybe he just wants to talk about the upcoming cruise?"

She shrugged. "The door's unlocked."

Dee rose and headed for their room.

———

WHEN DEE STEPPED INSIDE JAMAL'S EYES WERE CLOSED BUT opened immediately when he heard footsteps.

"Hey," he slurred.

"You okay?"

"Just a little groggy, but I wanted to talk to you before I slept too long and forgot what I wanted to say, or imagine I dreamed it."

"Okay, what's up?"

"When I fell, and I was looking up at the ceiling, I noticed the Armorial wasn't as deep as the Great Hall."

"That's what I thought you said." Dee nodded. "Why does it matter?"

"I don't know that it does. It was just the way the ceiling turned in and then away made it look like a corner, or another room, or that there was more space behind the painting of Alexander. That space would have made the room as deep as the Great Hall."

"How did you see that or know that?"

"When we crossed from the Great Hall into the Armorial I was looking at the far walls at the end of the room. I could see that the Armorial wall was closer. And then when I fell and was on my back looking up, I could see the ceiling turn in and then away as if there should be more space."

"Maybe it was just on the other side?"

"We just came from there. It was square. The walls should have been flush according to the map the guide gave us. There was no difference in the length leading back to the Small Throne Room."

"I don't know. What's your thought?"

"Not sure, something odd. Maybe it's just the way my head feels."

Dee paused for a moment, hesitant to tell Jamal what he'd seen in the lobby. "Do you remember the guard, or whatever he was, who helped you into the wheelchair?"

"Yeah, big burly guy in a blue blazer."

"Well, he followed us here, and he's down in the lobby. It looks like there may be a couple of other guys with him."

"What? Why would they follow us?"

"I've been asking myself that. At first I thought maybe they were just checking, to make sure you weren't hurt. You know bad for business, bad for the tourists. But with several of them, I don't know."

"We haven't done anything. Why would they care?"

The door opened, and Angelic and Gina walked inside. "Feeling any better, babe?"

Jamal nodded. "Yeah, maybe something to eat?"

"Let's go get lunch," said Gina.

———

Walking beside Jamal and the others on the way to the restaurant, Dee noticed the men watching them closely. The men made no attempt to conceal their surveillance.

After being seated, Jamal leaned in to Dee and said, "That was weird. They were just staring right at us."

After they finished lunch, the group went back to their rooms. The men were gone from the lobby. Jamal slept for the rest of the afternoon.

———

The next morning as the ladies prepared to go shopping, Jamal made a suggestion. "I'd like to go back to the museum for a minute, take Dee with me while the rest of you get started shopping. I just want to show him something I saw right before I fell. We'll be along shortly. Don't buy the place out, at least until I get back."

"You know we'll wait, you're paying," said Keno.

Dee pointed to Mike. "Keep an eye on them. We won't be long."

———

Slipping back inside the museum, they didn't attach to a group but made their way to the Armorial Hall and the Military Gallery. Passing into the Armorial from the Small Throne Room, they saw the guy from the day before. He was scanning the crowd but didn't make eye contact. *Well, it was his job.* Standing in the doorway looking back toward the Small Throne Room, the Military Gallery was definitely shorter than the Armorial. Jamal pointed out where the ceiling turned inward. Looking on the Armorial side, the ceiling met the walls at a ninety-degree angle.

"You're right. It looks odd. But maybe it's just an architectural detail of the period. I think there was a fire and some remodeling in the 1800s."

"Yeah, probably. I just wanted you to see it, so you'd know I wasn't hallucinating."

"Never doubted it. We'd better catch up to the group, before they buy out the whole store."

"Don't know what I was thinking, offering to pay."

Dee tapped him on the shoulder with a fist. "I don't know either, but I appreciate it."

They exited the palace and were in the garden heading for the gate entrance and the street. Coming out of a side door across the courtyard was the guy who had brought them the wheelchair. Looking back to the path they were on, there was another of the men from the hotel lobby walking toward them.

"Odd coincidence, don't you think?" whispered Jamal.

"Yeah, very," Dee replied and moved closer to Jamal so that they were shoulder to shoulder.

The two men approached, one from the side, one from the

front. That was when Dee and Jamal realized there was a third man behind them, effectively blocking their way.

"Can we have a word with you? Just take a minute," said the man who had approached from the front.

Dee and Jamal glanced at each other, then back to the man, and nodded.

"This way." He gestured with his hand.

"What's wrong with right here?" asked Dee.

"A little privacy, get out of the sun." He motioned again and started to walk toward a side entrance of the building. The other two men fell in, and Dee and Jamal had little choice but to follow the first man.

Once inside the small office, the leader motioned toward two chairs. Dee and Jamal sat down and then realized the other two men were now standing behind them.

Glancing quickly at the men, Dee said, "What is it you need?"

He pointed at Jamal. "We want to know what you said yesterday."

"Said about what?"

"When you were on the floor, Andrei heard you say something about the length of the rooms."

Jamal held his hands up. "I was just stammering."

"Then you came back today and were studying the rooms more closely. Who are you? What do you want? What is your interest here?"

Jamal looked at Dee, who spoke up. "We're just tourists. He was showing me an architectural detail he thought he saw when he fell. We just came back to quickly verify if he actually saw it."

"And?"

"And what?"

"This detail, what's so important about it?"

Dee paused, looking around at each of the men. "Nothing really. We were just curious."

"Not always a good thing." He stood up from behind the desk. "I don't believe you."

Suddenly there was a set of hands on both Dee's shoulders and Jamal's. They twisted in their seats but were quickly subdued.

"Don't make this more difficult," said the leader. "Tell us what you know."

"About what? We don't know what you're talking about."

The hands on their shoulders had gotten firmer and began to twist. Dee and Jamal were squirming in discomfort.

"Who do you work for?"

"We're retired tourists. We travel the world. We don't work for anyone."

The hands stopped twisting but held them firmly in the chair. "Perhaps. We have the names and likenesses of your whole group. Let's hope we see no other indication of this curiosity you display." The man turned and left the room.

———

A short time later Dee and Jamal found themselves deposited in the Raphael Loggia of the Hermitage. The two broad-shouldered men walked away without looking back.

"What could they have possibly wanted?" whispered Jamal.

"Apparently they think we know or saw something they don't want known or they want to know about."

"Something about the floor plan? Why would it matter?"

"I have no idea. Could they be hiding something?"

"The Revolution was more than a hundred years ago. What would matter now?"

"Something more recent perhaps?"

The men leaned back against the exterior wall. Jamal looked up and down the corridor. "These are reproductions of the Raphael paintings from the Vatican. Catherine the Great couldn't purchase them for her collection, so she had them recreated."

"What's your point?"

"I don't know. But there's something going on here. Diego told me about the Loggias, said they were an exact reproduction. As I'm sitting here and looking over at that column, I don't recognize the illustration. These are supposed to be Old and New Testament stories. But look at that," he said, pointing toward a near wall. "It looks more like a castle than a church and what is the gold wall?"

Dee looked at it. "Don't know. It wouldn't be a gold wall, not in the Bible."

"You're right. The scene doesn't look religious."

They examined the painting again. Beside it there was another painting, of a church.

"Wait, a minute. Let me take a picture," said Jamal. "Then let's get out of here." He snapped a shot, then another, and they hastily left the building.

———

Outside, sitting on a bench along the river, Jamal scrolled through his phone. After several minutes he stopped, looked up, and then spoke. "I compared the picture I took to the original murals in Rome, and there isn't one. That means it was added. It's something extra. Why would that be?"

"So did they intentionally drop us in front of it or not? What does that have to do with you falling and questioning the length of the room?" replied Dee.

"I doubt they intentionally dropped us in front of it. Just a coincidence."

"I don't know. A place as old as this probably has many secrets. But I think they're related."

"So what do we do?"

"I don't have the faintest."

"I love this stuff, but we're supposed to go shopping. Give me just a minute." Jamal went back to his phone and studied the photos he had taken. He held them different ways and studied the results. Then he blew the pictures up, reduced them back and stopped. He pointed the phone toward Dee. "What is that church? That's not an original either."

Dee glanced at the photograph. "That's the Church of the Savior on Spilled Blood. It's here in St. Petersburg."

"It's not on the original Loggia in Rome."

"No, it was built in the late 1800s by Czar Alexander III in honor of his father, Alexander II, who was assassinated on that spot."

"Long after the Loggia."

"Absolutely."

"Why would they add it?"

"I don't know but we can go take a look tomorrow before we board in the afternoon."

DEE & FRIENDS - READY TO SAIL

Dee and Jamal met the rest of the group at the GUM store. They had a massive pile of merchandise. Jamal just sighed and pulled out his black credit card.

Later that evening Jamal and Dee shared with the group what had happened at the museum.

"What could they have possibly wanted?" asked Gina.

"Were you hurt?" asked Angelic.

"Sounds like you were lucky," added Mike.

"We don't know what they want. Something about the comment I made regarding the rooms, specifically the walls being different lengths, seemed to be a problem for them," answered Jamal.

"Are they hiding something?" asked Mike.

"It's too bizarre. The fall, the ceiling, and then the paintings in the Loggia not being authentic and pointing to other churches. It definitely seems like there's something."

"It all sounds too fantastic," added Keno.

"There's that," replied Jamal.

Dee shared their plan for visiting the church in the morning. "Would anyone like to go with us?" asked Jamal.

"Sleeping in," replied Keno, followed by nods from Angelic and Gina.

"Are you sure you should be doing this?" asked Gina. "You guys need to be careful."

"I'll go," said Mike. "Just to see what you're up to. Keep you from getting in any more trouble."

———

THE FOLLOWING MORNING DEE, JAMAL, AND MIKE CAUGHT A cab for the church. The women promised to stay at the hotel, in their beds, until they returned.

Stepping out of the cab, the men glanced up at the façade of the Church of the Savior on Spilled Blood. It was massive, many stories high, wildly ornate, and topped with five onion domes.

"The czars didn't go cheap on anything did they?" said Jamal.

"Sure doesn't look it," replied Mike.

"Especially on monuments to themselves. Let's get started," added Dee. "We don't have that much time, and this place is probably chock full of murals."

Once inside, they realized the truth of Dee's words. The walls were lined from floor to ceiling with mural after mural stretching high into space.

"It'll take us all day," said Mike.

"We don't have all day," replied Dee.

"Okay, let's split up," said Jamal. "Mike we're looking for a scene that has a gold wall in a room. The wall looks like it's in sections. The surrounding structure seems more like a castle or some type of building other than a church. So far, the movement of the mural draws your eye to an adjacent mural of another church. That's what we're looking for."

Mike nodded. "I'll start at the bottom, you guys start at the top, since you know more what to expect."

Dee and Jamal nodded and each of them started in a different direction.

———

TWO HOURS LATER THEY HAD EXHAUSTED HALF OF THE IMAGES. They had gotten quicker. It was easier to spot a biblical scene, and they moved from image to image. They met together at the foot of one of the main interior walls.

"We're running out of time," said Jamal. "I've been thinking. It's not going to be prominent, because it's out of place. For the second half of the building let's start with the obscure corners or the out of the way halls. Something like that."

Dee and Mike nodded and split up again, moving quickly. Time was running out.

Forty-five minutes later Mike called the other two over to a far corner of the sanctuary on the back side of a column. There it was. The image depicted looking down into a four-walled room of golden panels in the interior of a building.

"We still don't know what or why," said Jamal.

"But we do know where to look next," said Dee. He pointed to the adjacent tile and there was a large multi-domed church, many stories high. Jamal took a quick picture. "It has an odd looking finish. I can't tell what it's made of."

"Let's get back to the hotel," said Mike. "We need to board soon. Jamal can look it up."

The three of them made their way to the front of the church. In a small corner behind where they had just stood was a large, short-haired man in coveralls, holding a broom. He didn't seem to be sweeping, but watching the three men leave the church.

———

They got back to the hotel in time for a late lunch and were joined by the ladies.

"How'd it go?" asked Angelic.

"Any trouble?" chimed in Gina.

"I think you're all crazy," added Keno.

Dee looked to Jamal who spoke. "We found what we were looking for."

"Another clue?" asked Angelic.

Jamal nodded.

"Which leads to another and another." Keno sighed, shaking her head at Mike.

"Hey," he replied, "I'm the one who found it. Least I could do after Jamal spent all that money yesterday."

"We board shortly. Is everybody ready?" asked Jamal, who was looking at his watch.

There were nods around the table as the men finished lunch.

"Is everybody enjoying their new stuff?"

There were smiles and thumbs up from everyone.

"Happy I could help."

———

They boarded that afternoon, and after the basic safety checks and introductions, unpacked in their staterooms.

Gathered in the Sky Bar, Jamal and Dee told the others the specifics of what they had found that morning and revisited the encounter with the men from the museum.

"What did they want?" asked Keno.

"We never did figure it out. Just glad to be moving on."

"So what was the significance of the mural you found this morning? It leads to another church?" asked Angelic.

"Is this some kind of wild goose chase?" asked Gina.

"We hope not," replied Jamal.

"Each mural seems to reveal a little more about this gold room," said Dee.

"Is it really gold or is that just the color?" asked Keno.

"Good question," replied Dee.

"Where are we headed?" asked Mike.

"Mandrogy, across Lake Ladoga, on the Neva River," replied Dee. "Then on to Kizhi on Lake Onega."

"The church we saw this morning, next to the gold room? I think it's on Kizhi Island," said Jamal. "And it appears to be wooden. One of the oldest churches in Russia. Hard to tell what the inside will be like."

"So the age of the church doesn't seem relevant. All these murals have been added at a later date in time," said Dee. "The one in the painting from this morning looks like the Church of Transfiguration of the Savior, which, as you said, is a wooden structure. One of the few remaining in the country. What do you think we'll find there?"

"Don't know. You wonder how long wood can hold up. Hopefully, the gold room or maybe another mural. But how does that relate to the hallway, or does it?"

"We'll take a look when we get there."

4

DEE & FRIENDS - DAY ONE

The following morning they were in Mandrogy after sailing all night from St. Petersburg.

Disembarking early in the day, they settled in to tour Mandrogy. It was only a half-day tour as it was a recreated historical Russian village. The original was destroyed in WWII and rebuilt in 1996 as a tourist trap. It consisted of shops, souvenirs, an inn, and a restaurant.

The island and village were quaint and the people friendly. But there was shop after shop. The women loved it. Each couple was paying for themselves today and the men reached into their wallets many times during the morning. Finally, they broke for lunch.

Coming in late, they were seated upstairs in the island restaurant. Shortly after sitting down and ordering, Dee, who faced the stairs, noticed something. The hostess was leading two large men, the men from the museum, across to the other side of the dining room.

Dee nudged Jamal, who was sitting beside him, with his leg. Then he leaned in and whispered, "Don't look now, but across the way are two of the three guys from the museum."

To Jamal's credit, he didn't look. But he leaned in closer and whispered to Dee, "You have to be kidding. Why would they be here?"

"Don't know, but it's them. Clearly they are following us."

"What do you want to do?"

"Let's see what they do. They want us to see them and presumably to be afraid. But why?"

Dee and Jamal finished lunch and, since the men had not moved or acknowledged them, without telling the others in the group, Dee and Jamal got up and walked over to the table with the two men. Each of them sat down beside one of the men.

"What a surprise to see you here," said Dee. "It's almost like you are following us. What's going on with that?"

The man closest to Dee just growled. The man across from him spoke. "We are following you. Because you are nosy and we want to know why."

"Why what?" asked Jamal.

The man looked down his nose, almost as if to spit. "You went back to the museum, and then you went to the church. You're looking for something."

"We're tourists. That's what we do, look at stuff," replied Dee.

"We don't think so."

"Why?"

"You act suspicious. Like you know something and we want to know what," he said, banging his fist on the table.

The restaurant got quiet.

"Perhaps we should take this outside," said the man who had not previously spoken.

"There's nothing to talk about," said Jamal.

"No, you will tell us." Each of the men grabbed Dee or Jamal by the arm and rose from the table. The nearest door led to a balcony. The men pushed it open and then spun Dee and Jamal against the rail while boxing them in with their bodies.

"We've got to stop meeting like this," said Dee.

"People will talk," added Jamal.

The men had their backs to the restaurant, with the door open. Dee and Jamal could see Mike quietly approaching.

Dee held his hands up, open palmed. "Look, we'll talk. Give us some space." Dee leaned back against the rail. The two big men relaxed their grips but didn't let go.

"It's like this," said Dee. He pulled away suddenly from their grip and shouted, "Over the side Jamal." Dee vaulted the rail and dropped to the ground, a story below. He rolled when he hit with Jamal right behind him. "Run."

The two Russian men gasped for a moment and as they went to turn, Mike hit them both like a battering ram from the backside. The men tumbled over the rail and landed clumsily on the ground, both of them groaning.

Mike went back to the women. "Let's go."

Back on the ship they met at the Panorama Bar so they wouldn't be outside and visible, but they could still see anyone approaching the ship.

"What happened?" asked Keno.

"They seem to think we know something or we're looking for something," replied Jamal.

"But we don't know what," added Dee.

"Maybe you know something and don't realize it," said Mike.

"Doesn't seem likely. This appears to have started when I fell. I don't know anything more now than I did then."

"They seemed interested, or maybe alarmed, when you talked about the room length. But then they followed us to the church, and that seems to have stirred them up more," said Dee.

"Don't see how those things can be related," replied Jamal.

"We only have four more days on this cruise. The sooner it's over and we get out of here the better," said Keno.

"I have to agree with that," added Angelic. "Whatever you're doing, you should stop it."

"The first church was in town and the second along the way. It didn't seem like it was a big deal to take a look."

"They seem to think it is," added Gina.

5

———————

DEE & FRIENDS - DAY 2

They woke up the next morning as the longship approached Kizhi Island. The church stood out like a golden thumb towering over the island and the short stand of greenery below. Drawing closer, they realized the greenery was from a fully grown stand of pine, and how tall and massive the church truly was. It dominated the landscape with twenty-one wooden domes. The structure below the domes was multiple stories high and seemed ancient in its frail gray coloring. Dee put a scope to it and realized there were spaces between the planks.

"It's a cold weather church," he called to Jamal.

Jamal turned to look at Dee, who continued. "There is no insulation between the planks that would catch moisture and cause the wood to rot. There's no heat source. It's probably used mostly in the summer. But that accounts for how many centuries the wood has lasted."

Jamal looked back to the church. "A gold room doesn't seem likely. If there are murals, they will be tile and not paint. Paint would never weather the cold for centuries. I hope we can find something."

As the ship pulled closer to the dock, a soft mist began to fall. Fog sprang up quickly and the lower level of the church was concealed.

"Can you imagine this place in the winter?"

"It would be so cold, nothing could survive."

They docked and, with big, bright red umbrellas the crew handed out, made their way along a wooden plank sidewalk to the visitor center outside the church.

They assembled by a guide. She began, "This island was once covered with churches and was thought of as a religious retreat. Most of them have been destroyed over time but the three that remain are prime examples. The largest, the Church of Transfiguration of the Savior, is the largest surviving wooden structure. It was built in 1714 as a symbol of Peter the Great's victory over Sweden."

It was raining harder now, and the umbrellas were scarcely adequate against the downpour. The guide looked at them questioningly.

Jamal rolled his hand in a circle. "Press on."

They made their way slowly along the trails between the buildings. Now there was thunder, but no lightning.

The guide stopped in front of the church. "The aspen wood used for the shingles turns black with moisture but dries out and returns to its normal golden yellow in the sun. The shingles are overlaid and slowly curved until the onion shape dome is realized."

We stepped inside and the walls were lined with tile mosaics. Jamal and I moved slowly and methodically around the room looking at each of them. The rest of the group followed the guide.

The murals lined the walls and columns of the structure as they made their way upward. They varied in size from 2'x2' to 3'x5' and were separated on the top and bottom by a row of decorative tile.

Each one that they looked at depicted a biblical scene. Moving slowly along, they hoped for something different. On the third wall, they saw the mural. The golden room, with a gold door, smaller and now inside a larger structure, but with no other identifying marks. The pattern of the tile swept down and to the right, leading the eye to the next tile. It was another church. Jamal quickly took a picture.

"It's not really an arrow, but it seems to point to that tile. Can we identify the church?"

"Probably, but what does it mean. The murals aren't telling us much."

Rejoining the group and finishing the tour, they returned to the longship.

"Did you learn anything?" asked Angelic as they sat in the Panorama Bar, inside from the weather.

Dee looked at her and grinned. "Yeah, it's cold and wet on that island."

Angelic punched him on the shoulder.

"Seriously?"

"Yeah," said Mike. "Out with it."

Dee looked to Jamal. "We found another mural that points to another church. The gold room was a little more detailed but we still can't tell anything about it. Where is it? What is it? Where to look? It's frustrating."

"You guys are always frustrated and looking for something," added Keno.

"Where is the next church and where are we going next?" asked Gina.

"I think Goritsy and Kuzino are the next stops. They are basically adjacent. It's a day and a half or so to get there. We cruise, stop and visit both, then sail on," replied Dee.

"Where's the church?" asked Angelic.
"I've got to research it," replied Jamal.

6

DEE & FRIENDS - DAY 3

They'd only been up for a few hours. The ship was now on Beloye Lake, another part of the Volga-Baltic waterway, which was really a series of lakes connected by short rivers or manmade canals. The group was standing at the rail watching the landscape slide past. Jamal was the first to see it. He had the scope and tried to zoom in on the structure.

"There. Looks like the remains of a building up ahead in the water, possibly a church."

"I hope it's not the one we're looking for," said Dee.

"If it is, we have a problem. Only the bell tower and part of the upper story are visible."

As they drew closer, all of them could see the remains. No roof, no windows, only walls remained. Jamal had handed the scope back to Dee and was flipping through his phone.

"I don't think that's it, but there's hardly enough remaining to tell."

"You may be out of luck," added Mike. "The search may be over."

"The picture of the structure looks larger. I think maybe

there's a church and a monastery that we are looking for. The picture is captioned in Russian and I can't get the 'translate' function to work."

"Let me try," said Dee. He reached in his backpack and pulled out a "Guide to Russian Churches."

"Where did you find that?" asked Gina.

"Surely you didn't own that?" added Keno.

"I found it in the ship's bookstore. Thought it might be helpful. Based upon Jamal's photograph, the church we're looking for is called the Kirillo-Belozersky Monastery and it's just beyond Goritsy."

———

SEVERAL HOURS LATER, AS THEY BEGAN THE FINAL APPROACH TO Goritsy, they saw a series of multi-domed spheres and a church that sat right at the water's edge.

The group was standing at the railing watching the town appear. "Is that it?" asked Keno, pointing toward the structure.

"I don't think so," replied Dee, staring at his book. "That is the Resurrection Convent, not a monastery. That would be nuns, we're looking for monks."

"Really," said Angelic, with a roll of her eyes. Gina giggled at them. "Please."

"The convent was founded by a daughter-in-law of Ivan the Terrible. She and her son, Ivan's grandson, attempted to have him overthrown. Ivan had the boy killed and sent the woman to be imprisoned at the convent she founded," added Dee.

"Ironic," said Jamal.

"Shortly after he sent her there, he had her drowned."

"I guess his name was well deserved," added Mike.

"So it would seem. Anyway, the monastery is just around the bend."

———

THEY DOCKED IN GORITSY IN A SMALL BAY ACROSS FROM THE convent and disembarked to tour the village. After a leisurely stroll across the town, they arrived at the monastery, which was on the next point along the river.

A guide met them at the entrance of the Kazan Tower.

Jamal stood looking around the structure as the others mingled. "This is really a fortress, much more than a church," he said to Dee.

"Yeah, do you think maybe the gold room could be here?"

"It might make sense, since it's heavily fortified. I'm still not certain what the murals are telling us."

"Maybe this time we'll get a better clue, or find it."

The guide waved her arms. "May I have your attention and we'll get started?" She began to walk through the gate. "This place was founded by two monks from Moscow. It was originally a hole dug in the ground and a large wooden cross. The monastery grew slowly but began to attract visitors, pilgrims if you will, and donors, in some cases large donors. It is said that Ivan the Terrible took a liking to the place and provided several very large contributions which helped with the rapid growth of the site. As you can see, it's quite large and once contained twelve churches."

Mike glanced at Jamal and Dee. "Maybe Ivan wasn't totally terrible."

"Maybe," replied Jamal. He then glanced at Dee. "How will we know which church?" asked Jamal.

Dee shrugged. "Keep listening and looking, hopefully your picture will help us narrow it down."

The guide resumed, "It was also said that Ivan the Terrible saw the location as being of strategic military importance, which led to his contributions and the twenty-three-feet thick walls you see surrounding the site." She pointed to the exterior walls around the perimeter. "Almost impregnable. For that day and time."

"Perhaps Ivan was just clever and not really kind or generous," said Mike.

"More likely," replied Jamal.

The guide led them into the Ascension Chapel. "The Bolsheviks abandoned the place in 1924 and only returned it to the Russian Orthodox Church in the 1990s. Much of the artwork is badly deteriorated. It was said that this site held one of the largest collections of early Russian religious artifacts. It's a shame. At its height, the monastery was the second largest landowner in Russia. But, Catherine the Great stripped many of their properties for the benefit of the throne. This place has had its ups and downs. Hopefully, the restoration that is currently underway will revive it."

"That's a bad sign," whispered Jamal. "We may not be able to recognize the next clue."

"Let's just keep looking."

They stopped in front of a wall mural and there it was.

"What does that look like to you?" asked Dee.

THEY STOOD BESIDE ONE OF THE BACK WALLS OF THE CHAPEL. It was crumbling at the top where it met the floor joist of the balcony above.

"Lots of water damage," said Jamal.

Dee nodded and pointed at the mural. It was paint not tile, and it was faded and watermarked in spots. But it was clear enough.

"That looks like it could be the Winter Palace," muttered Jamal.

"Could be," replied Dee, taking another step closer. "And there's a room with a gold door."

Jamal took a couple of steps to his right. The mural blended into a life-size portrait of a man. "Who is that?"

Dee took a quick look. "I'd guess it to be Peter the Great or maybe Ivan the Terrible."

"Wonder if that means anything?"

Dee shrugged. Jamal moved farther to the right. The portrait dissolved into another church. Jamal looked back at the portrait. The figure's hand was outstretched and pointed at the church.

Jamal turned to Dee. "Do you suppose there's more? And what does it mean about the gold door and the Winter Palace?"

"No idea. Take a picture and let's catch up to the group."

As Jamal snapped the picture, an older man in a rumpled khaki suit stepped up behind them. "There are no pictures allowed here," he said.

Dee and Jamal both turned. Dee spoke, "Sorry, we didn't know. We'll be on our way. Catch up to the tour."

They nodded at the man and quickly scurried away. Looking back, they saw him studying the wall mural of the Winter Palace intently.

"Who was that?" asked Jamal.

"He didn't look like the museum guys. Maybe one of their bosses?"

"Or someone the museum guys brought in to assist them?"

"That couldn't be good."

They caught up to the tour and spent the next several hours hiking about the grounds and inside the other remaining structures. Only once did they see the man in the khaki suit, and he was across the yard from them coming out of another building.

———

THE LONGSHIP HAD REPOSITIONED FROM GORITSY TO KUZINO, from one side of the two towns, where it had docked, to the other side of the town, where they now boarded. The group secured all their purchases in their staterooms and met in the Panorama Bar.

"Where did you guys get off to there for a while?" asked Keno

"We saw the mural we were looking for," replied Jamal.

"We may have learned something this time," added Dee. "The gold room appears to be in the Winter Palace."

"What does that mean?" asked Angelic.

"Real gold or gold colored or what?" added Gina.

"We don't know," replied Jamal.

"But it did point us to another church," added Dee.

"Of course it did," said Keno.

"Go easy on them," said Mike, looking in Keno's direction. She rolled her eyes at him.

"So, what are you going to do?" she added.

"We need to identify the church," said Jamal.

"And if the room is in the Winter Palace, we're going away from it, so hopefully there's no issue," added Dee.

Jamal turned to look at him. "But, when we stopped today to take the picture of the palace and the next church, there was a man," said Dee.

"He was older, about your height, in a rumpled khaki suit," said Angelic.

"How did you know that?" asked Jamal.

"I saw him watching us several different times. It seemed to be too much of a coincidence. I suspected it had something to do with you guys."

"Was he alone?" asked Dee.

"He appeared to be. I saw him moving about the grounds, didn't seem particularly interested in anything but our group."

"Any idea who he is?" asked Mike.

"We'd never seen him before and he didn't really look like the museum guys," replied Dee.

"Which could be good or bad," added Mike.

"I guess we wait and see," said Jamal. "Keep an eye out for him everyone."

7

DEE & FRIENDS - DAY 4

The ship cruised for a day to get from Kuzino to Yaroslavl. There were many churches along this stretch of the Volga. Dee and Jamal spent the day at the rail looking at Jamal's photograph, Dee's reference book, and every church they passed to see if it might be the one. Mike helped them spot for several hours. The ladies took advantage of the time and slept, read, and sat in the bar chatting. The river was broad, and the scenery was beautiful.

"I'd be enjoying this if we weren't working so hard," said Mike.

Jamal looked up at him, "Yeah, us too."

"The book says many of these churches were shut down in the 1920s and 1930s. They were left abandoned or used for other purposes," said Dee. "They weren't reopened until the 1990s. If it's any of them, the artwork is probably gone."

Jamal nodded. "Just our luck to get this far and not be able to go further."

They kept looking as the longship eased closer to Yaroslavl. On their left appeared a long structure with a bell tower and a cathedral.

"Could that be it?" asked Dee.

Jamal glanced at the picture. "I don't think so; the onion domes don't have the correct proportion or physical relationship. Look in your book."

Dee glanced quickly to the book. "It says that it's the Godenovo-Tolga Monastery." He continued to look at the book.

"So, not it. Something wrong?" asked Jamal when Dee continued to look at the book.

"No, it says here that a local lord, in the 1300s, camped there one night. The morning after, he woke up and told his men of a dream where he walked across a bridge to the far side of the river. There he saw a ball of flame and a portrait of the Madonna and Child. The group went to depart and the local lord couldn't find his cane. On a whim he sent his men to the other side of the river. There was no bridge. When they came back from the far side, they had his cane and a portrait, a painting, of the Madonna and Child that had been wedged in a tree. There was evidence of a large scorched spot on the ground."

"Seriously?"

"That's what it says. The local lord was so mystified that he ordered a church to be built on the spot of the scorched earth."

"Well, it doesn't look right, so I hope we're not dealing with something like that."

Standing at the rail watching the shore, they approached the city of Yaroslavl. "What kind of name is that?" asked Jamal.

Dee glanced back at the reference book. "It says here that Yaroslavl the Wise was a great leader from this area. He founded the town, and it was named after him."

"Reckon he was related to Ivan the Terrible? They had some colorful names."

"Maybe. I know most of the later monarchs were interrelated. I'm not sure how far back in time that goes."

"The book goes on to say that Yaroslavl, the town, is part of something called 'The Golden Ring.' It's a circle of cities, springing out from Moscow, that retain the flavor of Imperial Russia. It's based heavily around the Russian Orthodox faith and its churches, which is what defines the circle."

"So, you think that has something to do with the golden door? The golden circle, the churches, the clues in the churches?"

"Seems reasonable, we're headed for Uglich and then Moscow, which are other points in the circle."

"Yeah, but why is the gold room in the Winter Palace? Is that the Winter Palace? Is there something comparable in Moscow?"

"The Kremlin contains several palaces. Maybe it's one of those."

"I still can't help but think it looks like the Winter Palace. Like the song says:

'Stuck around St. Petersburg, when I saw it was time for a change,
killed the czar and his ministers, Anastasia screamed in vain.'"

*

"So you think its revolution related?"

"Yeah, I do. I just don't see the Soviets running around adding murals to churches and leaving clues to something."

"So this Golden Ring, it could be a thing?"

"Seems the most logical, if we can collect enough pieces to see if it fits."

———

*Lyrics from the song "Sympathy for the Devil" by Mick Jagger and Keith Richards (Rolling Stones)

8

DEE & FRIENDS - YAROSLAVL

They docked at Yaroslavl and disembarked to tour the city. It was to be all day.

"Why are we always walking?" asked Keno.

"What would you prefer, a golf cart?" Mike chuckled.

"That would work," Keno replied.

Mike took her by the hand. "Come on, it's good for you."

They trudged along with the group. The first stop was the Church of St. Elijah the Prophet. As they gathered at the doors and the guide droned on, Jamal turned to Dee and held up his phone. "This is it."

"Really, it was that simple?"

"You heard the guide. This is the most famous and oldest church in town. Seems like a logical place."

The guide interrupted their discussion as they moved through the front doors. "This church is lined from the floor up the walls and across the ceiling with murals. There are literally hundreds, if not a thousand or more, as many of them blend together. There aren't just biblical scenes or characters; there are many images from everyday life in the 17th century."

"This could be really difficult," whispered Jamal to Dee.

"We'll need the others' help. You think they'll be willing?"

"Perhaps if we incentivize it."

"That cost you a fortune last time."

"It's only money. This is a mystery. Much more exciting."

"Bless your heart."

They motioned the group away from the tour and told them their plan. "Just exactly what kind of incentive?" asked Keno.

"When we get to Moscow, pick out whatever you want."

"Seriously?" asked Angelic.

"That's too much," said Gina. "We're happy to help."

"We're looking for a piece of the puzzle," said Mike, who then turned to Keno. "You know I'll buy you whatever you want in Moscow."

"I was just having fun with him," replied Keno. "Now what are we looking for again?"

"A structure that looks like the Winter Palace, or something similar, with a golden door. Actually, any structure with a golden door and maybe a church in the panel next to it," replied Jamal. He pointed to the wall. "Many of these are adjacent or bleed into each other but some have those ornate columns or rows of highly decorated tiles between the images. Find the gold door first, then look around it to see what the nearby scenes contain. Let Dee or I know. And thanks for helping."

Keno gave him a nod. "These tours can get a little boring. This should spice it up."

Jamal assigned them each a different direction, and the search was underway. "Remember, we have to meet up out front in just over an hour."

The church was crowded, which helped them in not staying with the tour. But it was large enough they still had room to look. It was overwhelming. Up steps, down steps, around corners, up columns, across the ceiling, one mural bled into another.

They are so ornate and detailed; we will never find them, thought Angelic.

There are so many of them. This is impossible, thought Keno.

I'm going to go blind, thought Gina.

These guys are crazy. Talk about a needle in a haystack, thought Mike.

This can't be the right place; we'll never find this, thought Jamal.

The tour is going to move on before we find it, thought Dee. *But, it's like Jamal said earlier, it's got to be obscure. But everything in here runs together. It's all obscure.*

Over an hour had passed and the time for the tour to move on was fast approaching. Dee was about to pass from the main assembly into one of the smaller auxiliary chambers that lined one side of the church. There were three passageways, arched, about six feet in length. Dee stopped for a moment and thought about it. Most people would go through the main and largest passage. Others would more likely go to the right than the left, from the main assembly hall. Coming back it might be the other way, but coming back, most visitors would be leaving and probably in a hurry. Dee entered the left passage. It, like the right passage, was just wide enough for one at a time. In the middle of the passage he stopped and looked straight up, over his head.

There it was. The Winter Palace, with the Neva River beside it. None of the Kremlin palaces were next to a river. It had to be. Looking closer he saw a gold-colored door on one of the rooms. Dee followed the mural in that direction and it bled into the picture of a small church. Far smaller than anything they had looked for so far. It looked almost modern. Not glass and steel modern, but old schoolhouse, next to all the onion domes they had been looking for. Glancing at his watch, Dee saw that the tour group would be gathering out front. He quickly took a photograph of the palace and the church and headed for the front door.

Dee scrambled up to the group, the rest of them already there, as the guide spoke. "We're heading downtown for something a little different, a small church, a chapel."

"I didn't think the czars did anything small," said Mike.

"Maybe it's not a memorial," added Angelic.

The guide led the way to a tour bus that had appeared.

"See I told you there was too much walking," Keno announced to the group as she scurried aboard.

Once they were all seated, the guide began again. "We are headed for the St. Alexander Nevskiy Chapel. It's different in size from most of the churches we will be visiting. It was built in the late 1880s to commemorate the survival of Czar Alexander III and his family from a train wreck. That might explain why it is only a chapel and not a full-blown church, as none of the royal family died." She smiled.

"I didn't know Russians had a sense of humor," said Jamal.

"It's probably okay to laugh at the czars," replied Dee.

The guide continued. "It's a relatively simple chapel with a small assembly area and only a few pieces of art, murals to be exact."

"How are we going to get back to St. Elijah to look more?" asked Jamal.

"We don't have to," replied Dee as he pulled out his phone. He opened the pictures. "I got this right before we left. I think we're headed there now. It's a small church, right next to a mural of the Winter Palace." He handed the phone to Jamal and pulled the reference book from his backpack. He found the page quickly and there it was.

———

THEY MET OUTSIDE THE BUS AND JAMAL QUICKLY SHARED THAT Dee had found the mural at the last minute and this appeared to be where they needed to be.

"How lucky was that?" asked Keno

"Kind of unbelievable, but cool," added Gina.

"I can't explain, expect to say that clearly this is something that happened later in time, maybe Czar Nicholas II before he was killed. Maybe he or someone close to him saw it coming. It was a precaution or something. This is a relatively new church compared to all the others we have looked at and found clues within. It should be easy; the guide said there wasn't much art work. Everybody keep their eyes open."

The guide called out, "Shall we go inside, this shouldn't take long."

As they started toward the doors Keno said, "It's tiny. Why would anyone hide anything here?"

"People might not think to look in a small place, maybe," said Angelic.

Once inside, they fanned out and Gina quickly spotted the mural behind the entrance doors. Both murals were small, no more than 1'x1'. There was the gold door on the inside of a hallway and another multi onion-domed church with a bell tower that was slightly taller than the domes.

"Interesting that the mural didn't show the entire Winter Palace," said Mike.

"Not enough space maybe," replied Dee.

"Perhaps whoever did this assumed anyone following the clues would know the location by now and this is just to keep you moving along," said Jamal.

"Or it could be an enormous gag," added Keno. "Not that I want to throw shade on your adventure quest."

Mike and Jamal scowled at her. Dee grinned. "She could be right."

They began to re-board the bus. The guide grabbed the

microphone and began to speak. "We are now headed for the Dormition Cathedral. The original church was built in the 1300s."

Jamal had been looking through Dee's reference book. "That's it. That's the one we are looking for, onion domes and a small bell tower. That's got to be it. It makes sense. Whoever did this was moving across town."

"That would be convenient," added Dee.

"Yeah, but when are we going to learn something about the room or whatever it is? We can't just keep jumping from church to church. It doesn't make sense."

"Perhaps it's a test of some kind?" said Dee.

"Or a fool's errand," said Jamal. "It's beginning to feel that way."

"If you've got the church identified, let's take a look. We're on a tour. We were going to these places anyway," replied Dee.

"You guys never give up," said Keno.

"What else did we have to do?" replied Jamal.

9

DEE & FRIENDS - YAROSLAVL - THE PARK

The bus made the turn from a crowded city street into the entrance of a park. At the end of the drive sat a large white church with golden onion domes and a small bell tower.

"It looks like you were right," said Dee to Jamal.

"I hope the next clue is as easy to find."

As the bus pulled to a stop, the guide made an announcement. "We are here now at the Dormition Cathedral. There in front, at the entrance to the walkway, you will note the two sculptures, the World War II monuments. One is of a Soviet soldier and the other is of a Soviet peasant. It's complete with an Eternal Flame. The Soviets were known for installing lots of public art, much of it in a severe style."

"There, she made fun of the Soviets too," said Mike.

"She's subtle but bold," said Angelic, as they all disembarked from the bus.

The tour approached the structure from the west side but stopped only momentarily before the guide led them around to the south side and the main entrance. As they stood before the stairway and grand entrance, the guide began again.

"This church was originally built in the 1300s and then rebuilt a number of times over the next five hundred years. But in a brief uprising against the Bolsheviks in 1918, the structure was heavily bombed. It was rebuilt somewhat during the 1920s but then torn down completely in the late 1930s under Josef Stalin's orders. It was not rebuilt until 2004."

Dee turned to Jamal and the others. "It can't be this one, or if it was, any clue is gone now."

Jamal's face grew long. "I'm sorry, baby," said Angelic.

"Tough break," added Mike.

Keno didn't speak but touched Jamal's arm.

"Are you sure this is it?" asked Gina.

Jamal nodded but Dee pulled his phone out to look for the pictures he had quickly taken at the Nevskiy Chapel and then to his reference book.

Dee looked at the photograph and then at the book. Then he looked at the photograph again and the book again. Then he expanded the photograph and slowly counted the number of onion domes, noting the placement and relationship to one another, and finally the bell tower. "I don't think this is it. The bell tower and the size and relationship of the domes isn't quite the same as the photograph."

"It probably wasn't rebuilt exactly the same," replied Jamal.

"That seems possible," added Mike.

"New guys, you know like the architects and engineers, are always changing stuff," said Keno.

"It's too bad," added Gina.

They were standing outside the south entrance looking at one another when Jamal said, "I don't even want to go inside."

There was a walkway leading away from the south entrance that appeared to lead into a small park. There were benches a short way down the path.

Angelic suggested, "Let's go sit there for a few minutes."

The group made their way to the benches and sprawled about.

Dee and Jamal were talking quietly while Mike listened. The women were grouped together and began chatting about what activities were left for the day.

Angelic looked up and toward the church. Gina and Keno were chatting about dinner. Angelic went to turn back but then she saw him. An older man, in a rumpled khaki suit. She'd seen him before at the monastery. Sitting there, trying not to look directly at him, because he was looking directly at them, she called to Dee and Jamal without moving her head.

"Hey guys, hey!" They turned toward her, their backs to the church. "That guy in the khaki suit from the monastery is over by the church."

"How do you know that?" asked Jamal.

"He's got a khaki suit on, and I recognize him. He's staring at us."

"Everybody stay in place," said Dee. "Keep doing what you're doing. Can you follow him with just your eyes?"

"Yes, he isn't moving." They sat for several minutes.

————

THE GUIDE EMERGED FROM THE CHURCH AND THE REMAINDER of the tour group collapsed around her as she started down the path toward where Dee and the others were sitting. As the tour passed, they blended into the middle of the group. As they approached the end of the path, there was a gazebo on a small point that overlooked the river.

"I didn't realize that we'd gotten back to the river," said Dee.

"I guess the town just wraps along beside it," replied Jamal.

The guide broke in over their discussion. Pointing at the gazebo she said, "This gazebo is often called the 'Temple of

Love' as many residents and tourists take romantic pictures, propose, exchange wedding vows, or hold wedding receptions. It's quite scenic and overlooks where the Kotorosi River converges with the Volga. Get your cameras ready." She led the way.

———

Suddenly there were two vehicles pulling in from the side, large black SUVs that came screeching to a halt with doors being flung open. Big, burly men, the men from the museum, and others emerged from the vehicles.

Dee pulled the group together quickly. "Everybody stick with the tour. Mike, you keep watch. Jamal and I will lead them away. Or at least see if they follow us." He turned to Jamal. "Run toward the park beyond the gazebo and away from the church. Let's start out together and see if we need to separate. Go!"

They sprinted toward the gazebo. Getting closer, they jumped a metal wrought-iron bench, ran across the gazebo floor, and vaulted over its rail to run down the side of the hill to the park below.

Back at the top, the men from the SUVs surrounded the tour, and the leader pointed at a couple of them and growled, "Hold them here, while we go after the others."

The tour guide exclaimed, "What's the meaning of…"

The leader growled again, "It's a matter of the State," and the guide fell silent for a moment. Then she turned, pulled a loose strand of hair behind her ear and said to the tour group, "Let's stand here a moment and let these men take care of their business. I suspect it will be over shortly."

The tour group turned as a whole to watch the men from the SUVs pursue the two men from their tour group that had vaulted the rail of the gazebo and were fleeing down the hill.

Angelic had been watching the men surrounding the tour group and turned to look for Jamal and Dee. In her peripheral vision she saw the man in the khaki suit running down the hill from farther back, closer to the church. She turned to Gina, Keno and Mike. "Look, it's the man in the khaki suit. He's following them too."

"That can't be good," said Mike, looking toward the men who stood guarding the tour group, and were now standing still, waiting to see what happened next.

"Do you think we could slip away?" asked Angelic.

"I doubt it. We're probably safer here in the crowd since it's mostly foreigners, although those guys don't seem to be bothered by stopping us."

———

DEE AND JAMAL WERE HALFWAY DOWN THE HILLSIDE AND COULD clearly see the park below.

"This runs out to a point in the river. We're trapped," said Jamal.

"Yeah, I know. We're just making it interesting for them, to see how bad they want us. They'd catch us no matter what."

"You're crazy."

"I've been told that. Keep running. Head for that statute at the end of the point. I see a crowd; maybe that will help."

They reached the bottom of the hill and started to sprint across the lawn.

"You sure this isn't going to just piss them off?" shouted Jamal as they ran.

"It probably will, but maybe their frustration or anger will get us some answers."

"Or get us beat to a pulp."

"There's that."

Jamal sped up. "I bet my forty time is better than yours."

"Yeah, but that's a quarter of a mile and I bet my quarter is better than yours."

"We'll find out." They both sped up.

———

FROM UP ABOVE ANGELIC COULD SEE BOTH OF THEM SPEEDING up, but they had nowhere to go. *What are they doing?*

She could see the men in pursuit had reached the bottom of the hill and were about forty yards behind Jamal and Dee. *It won't be long now. I hope they don't get killed. I'll never be able to explain this to his parents.*

Far to the side she could see the man in the khaki suit approaching from another angle. He didn't seem to be with the men from the SUVs. They were approaching from different directions. Khaki suit had dropped back so as not be in the line of sight of the pursuing men. Angelic doubted they knew the man was there.

"They're going to run out of space soon," said Mike. Gina and Keno were on tiptoes trying to watch.

"Are they gaining on them?" asked Gina.

Mike nodded but didn't reply.

"That's Yaroslavl Park. The statue is of Yaroslavl the Wise, and around the base it tells about the city," said Gina.

Keno turned to look at her. "How would you know that?"

"I read it in Dee's book."

———

DEE AND JAMAL INTERSECTED THE PATHWAYS THAT WERE THE last stretch to reach the statue.

"Almost there," said Jamal.

"Let's slow down and walk the rest of the way."

"You tired?"

"No, they should reach the point about the same time we do, but we'll look like tourists that just walked up and they will be the ones causing all the commotion. Might play in our favor. We've got to hope the crowd isn't locals and won't be intimidated."

"So you play a lot of chess?" asked Jamal.

"Once upon a time. Here we go." Dee broke into a stroll as they reached the sidewalk. He took a quick look over his shoulder. "They're coming."

"Quickly," added Jamal.

———

"They're walking," said Mike.

"What?" asked Angelic.

"Dee and Jamal are on the sidewalk near the statue and walking toward it. The men are still running after them. What's going on?" said Mike.

"Look," said Angelic. She pointed at the man in the khaki suit who was approaching the statue from an angle. Suddenly he stopped and blended into a tree and disappeared.

"That's weird," said Keno.

"It's like he's hiding too," added Gina.

"Or he's watching," said Mike. "We don't really know who he is."

———

Dee and Jamal reached the statue and stopped in front of it, facing each other and able to see over their shoulders as the men approached.

"Won't be long now," said Dee.

"I'm going to let you talk," replied Jamal. "I never played much chess."

As the men approached and slowed down, Dee whispered, "Here we go."

The four men surrounded them on three sides from about six feet away. The biggest of them took one step closer. "We should kill you right here."

Dee looked up at him, surprise on his face, "Whatever for? Who are you? My friend and I just wanted to see the statue and decided to have a race. Where did you come from?"

The man took another step forward, his fist clenched. "I'd prefer you dead, but Moscow station wants to talk to you."

"Who?" said Jamal.

"You've been snooping around the Winter Palace and the churches. Places you don't belong. They want to know why. You will be coming with us."

Suddenly there was a little red dot on the side of the man's head. He froze.

Dee and Jamal took another step back, closer to the statue.

A voice called out. "You and your men need to walk away or I'll spray your brains all over the base of that statue. Hands where I can see them and off you go."

The big man paused for a moment as if thinking, but then turned slowly and nodded, his hands in the air. He gestured to his men.

The voice called out again. "Before you go, let me hear you tell your men up top that there are car bombs on your SUVs and that they need to just walk away from the tour group and keep on walking. I'll hold the scope on you until you get back to the top and I see the tour group move on. Be moving along."

The big man spoke quickly in Russian into his ear mic and then nodded his head. "It is done."

"Start walking." The big man and his comrades slowly began their way toward the gazebo.

The voice called out again. "Stay where you are for now."

Dee and Jamal both nodded. They stood where they were for nearly ten minutes as the big man and his crew walked across the park, up the steps, and onto the road. The tour group began to descend the steps without any of the additional security men.

The voice called out once again. "Let the tour group get a little closer. I can still see the men but they are moving away."

Dee and Jamal stood another five minutes as the tour group approached.

10

DEE & FRIENDS - THE INTRUDER

And then, there he was. The man in the rumpled khaki suit standing beside them.

He stuck out his hand. "My name is Dimitri Kuznetsov, and we need to talk."

He was older than they had originally thought. They had only seen him in dim light and from a distance. He still moved like a young man but he was older, worn, and maybe weary.

"We have more people in the tour group," said Dee.

"Yes, I know," replied Dimitri. "I'm sure you will all have questions. I'd suggest we get away from here quickly. By the way, the church you're looking for is across the Kotorosl River." He pointed.

Dee and Jamal looked up beyond the Yaroslavl statue and there it was—the domes and the bell tower they had been looking for.

"It's on the other side and is called the Church of Saint John Chrysostom."

"How did you know?" asked Jamal.

"I've been following you since the monastery. I knew there

were clues in the murals, I just didn't know what they were or where to start. That church has the correct number of domes and relationship to the bell tower of the mural we saw at St Alex's Chapel."

Mike and the women walked up as the tour group surrounded the statue. "We saw what you did," said Mike. "We want to thank you, but what's your story?"

"Now that you are all here, let's walk. We need to get away from this place." They started back toward the gazebo. "We can arrange transportation for you back to the ship. You should be safe there."

"What about the church?" asked Jamal, looking over his shoulder.

"We can check tomorrow," said Dimitri.

"Who are you? Why should we trust you?" asked Dee. "You saved our lives, but that could have been an elaborate setup. What's the big secret here that everyone seems to think we know? Those guys gave up really easy."

Dimitri slowed his walk and turned to the group. "Those guys are a lot like our government. They're worker bees, they aren't going to die for anything, unless they're forced."

"Our government?" asked Mike.

"Yeah, I'm an American citizen, with Naval Intelligence," replied Dimitri.

"Ours or theirs?" asked Dee.

"Both. That's one of the reasons I want to keep moving. I'm first generation, but my father and grandfather were Russian. I'm fluent and I've spent a lot of time in this country. They think I'm a defector and a double agent. I'm actually a triple. But I'm here with you because of my family."

"Your family?" asked Gina.

"It's a long story. Let's get someplace safe."

As they neared the end of the sidewalk, Dimitri pointed to some landscaping. He stopped. "Let's stop for a moment.

Here's an FYI," he said. "The greenery there in the shape of a bear is the symbol of Yaroslavl. The '1009' is the year the city was founded. Yaroslavl was the Russian Daniel Boone. He killed the bear, and they named the city after him."

Dee and Jamal were looking at him blankly.

Dimitri spoke again. "The big guy from the statute is in a small powerboat in the river behind you. He looks to be alone and seems to be going away, toward that dacha on the hill. It must be a safe house or a meeting place for his group."

"Who is he with?" asked Jamal.

"One of the security services out of Moscow. It doesn't really matter. They can all arrest you or kill you with no questions asked or answered."

Dmitri pointed between them. "Look, he's in a golf cart riding up that winding drive. It's only him, wonder where his men are? We'd better get moving. See how's its clear cut from the river up the drive and around the dwelling? It's definitely a secure location. I'll research it later tonight."

THEY WERE IN THE PANORAMA BAR ON THE LONGSHIP. THE crew had let Dimitri board with them as the ship was docked in Yaroslavl for another night. They gathered around a large table in a corner of the bar.

"So tell us what's going on," said Dee.

"I don't know why security is following you," replied Dimitri. "I saw a bulletin they issued talking about some curious tourists in the Winter Palace. There was no reason or definition given for why they called you curious. But it piqued my curiosity. So I began following you. Once I saw you were on track of the murals in the churches is when I got really interested."

"Why is that?" asked Angelic before Dee or Jamal could get out the question.

"It goes back to my grandfather who was a pastor late in his life for the Russian Orthodox Church. He was in a small rural location outside St. Petersburg."

"I thought you were an American," said Keno.

"I am. Let me start there and we'll work our way back to my grandfather and why I'm hoping you can, or will, help me."

———

HE LOOKED AROUND THE GROUP; THEY WERE ALL WAITING.

Dee interjected. "We don't really know anything. It's like we have a couple of pieces of a puzzle, maybe, which we discovered by accident. We're on this river cruise, so far we've been able to coordinate the two—the trip and the search, if that's what it is."

"Okay, let me start with my father and tell you my story. My dad was in the last graduating class of the czar's naval academy in 1917. His name was Mikhail Kuznetsov."

"Your father graduated in 1917?" asked Gina.

Dimitri smiled. "Yes, but let me continue. He was commissioned early in that year and assigned to a Russian ship that was in the Philippines when the Bolsheviks overthrew the government. He was a junior officer and went AWOL from the ship when they got the news. He hung around Manila for a few years running a ferry business. On one of his charters there were American Naval officers. They got to talking and were impressed with his background. The officers helped him get to America and by World War II he was commissioned in the US Navy, where he eventually rose to the rank of Captain. He was wounded late in the war in the Sea of Japan. Russians never liked the Japanese anyway, long history of conflict, so he was happy to be there. Anyway, he was decorated with a Navy Cross and a Purple Heart. There was some publicity and once he mustered out, he was the first man offered the captaincy of a Standard Oil tanker running from the Middle East to the US refineries. He captained them for most of the 1950s, got married and had a family, a boy and two girls."

———

It is the summer of 1952. I am honored to captain the first oil tanker to the Middle Eastern oil fields. I was lucky to survive the Second World War and to serve in the American military after being trained in the czar's Navy. But then I did desert and took a long road to this country. I wish my father could join me.

I am Mikhail Kuznetsov. I am a lucky man.

———

"That's you?" asked Angelic.

"No, they were my half-brother and sisters. They've all passed. As did my father's first wife. In the early 1960s he had to retire and needed home health care shortly afterwards. My mother was his caregiver. He was 68 when I was born."

"I guess he got some really good care," said Mike.

"My mom was 28 years younger and wanted to have a child. She had lost her husband early in her life."

"So here you are," said Gina.

Dimitri nodded. "I joined the Navy when I was old enough. But before that, Dad had told me lots of stories from the days of the czars up to the oil tankers. We lived on the shores of Lake Michigan and he got strong enough that he taught sailing. On a sloop, nothing big. He was in his seventies by this time. I was eight. We were out one day and he dropped me on the dock to run into the store to get us something to drink. He was fiddling with the sails. When I came back out I saw two men had approached him. I hid behind a cooler where they couldn't see me but I could see and hear them."

"What made you stop?" asked Mike.

"To this day I couldn't tell you. I just did."

———

It is the summer of 1972. I'm finally old enough to sail with father. He seems so frail sometimes. I hope we have more time together. I want to be a good sailor like him. He says he was in the czar's Navy. I'm not quite sure what that is but I've seen uniforms in the house and Mom says he was wounded in the war. I want to hear his stories.

I am Dimitri Kuznetsov, and I will be a good sailor.

———

It is the summer of 1972. My son is finally old enough that we can do things together. He is learning and one day will make a fine sailor. We have had such fun on the Great Lakes this summer. I look forward to watching him grow and become a man.

I am Mikhail Kuznetsov. I am a lucky man and I have lived a long life.

———

"So what happened next?" said Keno.

"There were two of them. One looked to be Dad's age or thereabouts, but the other was younger. I can't say for sure because when you're eight years old anyone over ten looks old. But he was a mean-looking man. I remember it so well because it was like I was seeing him in slow motion, him and the events that followed."

Everyone leaned in a little closer as Dimitri paused and caught his breath.

"He wasn't as tall as Dad or the other man, probably medium height. He had a thick, muscled build, broad shoulders, and swarthy skin. His nose was crooked, and his eyes were jet black. He had a long gray-black beard and thick, greasy, silver hair held by a band of some kind, like you might see on a young girl. When he spoke, I saw his mouth move and he had stained, gnarled teeth. He pointed a short stubby finger at my dad. And then there was a dagger. It was a shiny bright thing with a long blade that glittered in the sun, colored stones on the handle. He stabbed my father through the heart and then slashed his neck as Dad fell toward the deck."

Everyone sat back, and there was a collective sigh.

"Right before Dad was stabbed, I heard him say 'My father (my grandfather) never told me.' Which seemed to infuriate both men and led to the attack."

"What happened? Did they see you?" asked Gina.

"I stayed hidden. I bit my hand to keep from screaming or crying out. A man came out of the store and yelled at them as my dad fell. The swarthy men released the dagger and he and the older man ran down the dock. The dagger hit the rail of the sloop and bounced back inside. When the man from the store ran after them, I grabbed the dagger. Would you like to see it?"

"You have it?" said Keno.

"It's what set me on this quest." Dimitri reached for the backpack he had brought from the car. He pulled the dagger out and unwrapped it for them.

Everyone leaned in but no one touched the dagger. It had a gem-encrusted golden handle and a long steel blade that looked sharp.

"That looks really unusual," said Dee. "Are the gold and the jewels real? Where did it come from?"

"You're correct. As best I can tell it came from the Imperial Russian coat of arms behind the throne in the Winter Palace. I've researched it and gone to the palace to look at the coat of arms and in some of the early drawings there appears to be a dagger, which is not there now."

11

DEE & FRIENDS - THE RIDDLE

"How do you explain that?" asked Jamal.

"I don't. It's just one of the pieces that I'm trying to put together."

"What about your grandfather? You said there was more to the story," said Gina.

"That's right. That's the other piece that I have. My grandfather, Konstantin, became a pastor or a priest in the Russian Orthodox Church late in his life. He was married and had a family, including my father, but the church allowed him into the priesthood with the stipulation that if anything happened to his wife, he could not remarry. They were assigned to a small rural church outside St. Petersburg. It turned out this church was located in part of a circuit which the royal family would ride in a carriage or on horseback. They often stopped at the church and my grandfather got to meet them. But the crux is that on one of the trips, Anastasia was in the graveyard looking at something and stumbled in a hole. My father picked her up and carried her inside where he braced her ankle. The czar was grateful, and that's ultimately how my father got into the Naval Academy. But, my grandfather and

Anastasia became friends and she would come to see him, sometimes with her family and sometimes on her own. He warned her it would be trouble if she was caught, but she persisted."

"Wasn't the whole family killed by the Bolsheviks?" asked Angelic.

"Yes, they were carried away from the palace and held for some time before a decision was made. None of the other royal families came to their aid, even though they were all related by that time. When the Bolsheviks went to kill the family, they weren't very effective and Anastasia and her brother, who was actually rather sickly, escaped. The brother was killed shortly afterwards but Anastasia eluded them for a time. She was headed for the church when they caught and killed her, almost at my grandfather's feet. Before she was killed she rolled a pearl Fabergé egg to my grandfather, who hid it from the soldiers that were following her."

"What did he do with it?" asked Keno.

"That's another part of the story that I don't know. My father thought my grandfather held on to it but never confirmed that. He, my father, believed that my grandfather thought he was protecting the egg and that the Romanoffs would return to power, which of course they never did."

———

It is the summer of 1920. The czar and his family are dead. The Romanoffs will not be returning to the throne. What must I do with the egg? Surely the Bolsheviks will not retain power for long and I can return the egg to a rightful heir. In the meantime I must keep it safe.

My son, Mikhail, was in the Philippines with the Imperial Navy. I have not heard from him. There were rumors the crews abandoned ship. I wish I knew his fate. I wish I knew my own.

My name is Konstantin Kuznetsov and I am a priest in the Russian Orthodox Church.

IT IS OCTOBER 1927. IT HAS BEEN TEN YEARS SINCE THE GREAT *revolution and the establishment of the state. I have searched for the pearl all of that time.*

I was accused of stealing it but was able to defend myself. No one missed the dagger from the Imperial Crest so frustrated were they by the errant pearl. Anastasia or one of her family took it. Of that I am sure. When the men finally captured and killed her outside the church, there was a rumor of something rolling across the ground toward the priest. No one followed it up at the time or connected it to the pearl. It was nearly a year before I pieced the story together and went to see him, the priest. He was full of platitudes and lies. It was clear by then that the revolution had succeeded and that the Romanoffs would not be returning. I felt confident he kept the pearl for himself.

I had him, his church, and his quarters searched but to no avail. His son was an officer in the Imperial Navy but deserted during the revolution. I suspected the priest had gotten the pearl to him somehow. But it never appeared again.

Then I beat him. But the priest would not talk. He would only say, when asked if he had it, that he did not know what I was talking about. That is not a denial; that is a misdirection.

I am Sergei Dimitrov, and I will find the pearl.

"SO HOW CAN WE HELP YOU?" ASKED JAMAL. "WHAT MAKES you think anything we've done or seen or know is related?"

"There was a Russian security minister named Sergei Dimitrov, a very powerful man, one of the original revolutionaries, who hunted the missing pearl for years. I suspect he was the older man on the dock with my father, and that they were questioning him about my grandfather who had been dead since the mid-1950s, also suspiciously. Apparently they thought he might have told my father something. Dimitrov is dead now too, but the man who was with him on the dock has taken his place as the head of one of the security agencies. He and I are the last living links. He's still looking for the pearl and so am I. Not for the pearl, but for what, if anything, it can tell us."

———

It is the summer of 1955. I am a high-ranking official in the Russian State Security Service. I have had a good career, yet rumors still circulate among the older leaders and original revolutionaries that I took the pearl from the throne of the czar. But, my years of service and my brutality have served me well. The rumors are not loud or rampant. Yet they persist and I continue to search for the pearl.

I'm going to see the priest one last time. He will tell me everything he knows. I have waited long enough. It is time for the pearl to be returned to its rightful place.

He was transferred from the St. Petersburg church to the Monastery of St. Nicholas for a short time and then to St. Basil's here in Moscow. He must have it with him. He must keep it close. I have forcefully searched every place he has lived.

I found him in his quarters in the bottom of St. Basil's. He steadfastly maintained no knowledge of what I was asking. He will make that claim no more.

I am Sergei Dimitrov, and I will find the pearl.

———

It is the summer of 1955. I am an old man and I grow weary. The Church has little use for me and I am shuttled around from location to location. At last I am here in St. Basil's, where they send old priests to die.

My one son, Mikhail, who was in the Imperial Navy, did survive and lives in America. He has invited me to come and stay with him. It is not possible for me to leave.

Sergei Dimitrov has haunted me for decades, searching for the egg. It has not been easy to protect. Several times I thought he would surely find it. I wish I had never laid eyes on the thing. But, Anastasia gave her life for it. I cannot waver. I must be strong.

I hear noises, someone comes now…

I am Konstantin Kuznetsov, a priest in the Russian Orthodox Church.

———

"WHAT'S HIS NAME? DID YOU EVER LEARN?" ASKED JAMAL.

"Oh yes, he's still around. His name is Novak Novachek. He was Dimitrov's assistant for many years and took his place when Dimitrov died."

"What was their relationship?" asked Mike.

"Not clear, there were rumors over the years, but the one certain thing was his loyalty to Sergei."

———

IT IS THE SUMMER OF *1972. I* GROW OLD AND WEARY. THE PEARL *has not emerged. Perhaps the royal family did abscond with it.*

I am mentoring a young man. Not really young, but strong of will and ruthless. He is a good companion. He believes in the cause and has no remorse in serving it. His name is Novak, which means the 'new' one. It suits him well.

As I study the history of the pearl, l think of the priest's family. I've always suspected the son, the deserter. Perhaps it is time to talk with him. I will take Novak and travel to America. We will talk with the son there. I will take the czar's knife and he will tell me the truth.

The son was not hard to find. He hadn't even changed his name. His wife and his children are dead. He is the end of the line. He will tell me.

I am Sergei Dimitrov, and I will find the pearl.

———

IT IS THE SUMMER OF 1972. I WAS LUCKY. SERGEI DIMITROV *plucked me from an obscure Russian fishing village in the far north. He needed some help, no questions asked. I helped him. Now I am his assistant and his friend. We are going to travel to America in search of a pearl egg that belonged to the former czar. Sergei was unjustly charged with stealing it, but someone in the royal family took it before they were killed. We will find it and clear his name.*

I am Novak Novachek and I will not fail my mentor.

———

"IS THE PEARL THAT VALUABLE?" ASKED DEE. "I'M SURE IT'S worth a great deal of money but why would someone, or some group, hunt for it for over one hundred years? What else is there about it?"

"It's a Fabergé original, one of only two ever made. To the right person it has enormous monetary and possibly historical value. But there's no definite answer. The legend, or the rumor, is that it contains a piece of information about some hidden wealth of the czars. The state is always interested in the czars and in wealth. My dad once told me that my grandfather had told him that Anastasia had once mentioned something about paintings or murals in various churches containing clues. That her father, Nicholas II—the last czar, had craftsmen augment existing artwork with these clues. It was a way to protect some information or treasure in the event something happened, but to leave a trail for any of them that survived. Nicholas II's wife, Alexandra Feodorovna, had a premonition that the family would be harmed and she had the pearl Fabergé eggs placed on the arms of Nicholas II's throne. One of those is supposedly what Anastasia rolled to my grandfather just before her death. The other is still in the Hermitage Museum."

"How did you piece all of that together?" asked Angelic.

"A lot of it is public knowledge, at least in various forms. I knew a part of it from my family, and I added scraps of other information that I turned up. Some of it is speculation. The public stories vary widely. I listened to them all and then sorted through them as best I could. I am an intelligence officer, albeit a low level one, which has been good. No one pays much attention to me. But I don't have access to many things, here or in Washington. I'm nearly retirement age or maybe I'm just tired. I'd quit them both if I thought I'd survive, but this mystery keeps me going, for now."

"You didn't tell us how we can help," said Dee.

"You seem to have stumbled on to something about the murals. Clearly from what I've seen following you, there's some indication of gold or a gold door or something in the Winter Palace, which makes sense for a location. Do you know anything more specific?"

"Only what you just said," replied Jamal. "We didn't know about the pearl, and I'm not sure about why they got so excited when I fell in the Winter Palace."

Everyone sat back for a minute. "I didn't really believe they were on to anything other than some kind of oddity," said Keno. "Then they kept going from church to church, but that scene they keep seeing could be anything."

"I would have agreed until those men showed up in the park this afternoon. I was beginning to wonder myself if there was any real correlation. I mean it was a story, about the murals, that was third or fourth hand at best. The czar may have been teasing his daughter for all I know. But today, that feels different. I'm going to go check the safe house. You stay on board until you hear from me."

"Will you go to your office and do computer stuff and pull up the details?" asked Gina.

"I wish it was that simple. Like I said, I'm low level, I don't have access. Even if I did, every keystroke in the state system is logged. It's foolproof. And they come around every so often and ask about certain research you have done. It's impressive. They can't always feed the people but they know exactly what you are looking at. I'll have to do this the old fashioned way. But I am an intelligence agent, not a spy, at least as far as they're concerned. I'll go on foot and check the house out tonight."

"Do you need help?" asked Dee.

"No. If you should be caught, no one would ever see you again. I can come up with some plausible excuse. But, I don't plan on getting caught. I'll talk to you in the morning, and we can go look at the church."

He got up to leave. Dimitri nodded all around. "Stay on the ship until we have a better idea of what's happening."

———

They ate dinner quietly and then met in Dee and Gina's room.

"Do we believe him?" asked Mike.

The women all nodded. "That story's too fantastic, plus what good are we to him otherwise?" said Angelic.

"I think he's real. I just don't know if we can help him," said Dee.

"We have so little to go on. I hope the church tomorrow will tell us something more."

"Everybody get a good night's sleep. We'll pass on the tour tomorrow, at least until we hear from him," said Dee.

12

DIMITRI - THE SURVEILLANCE

Dimitri waited until 3am in the morning. He knew that 4am was the time of deepest sleep. He made his way to within a half mile of the dacha, then parked the car and walked in from there. The tree line and clear ground put him even further from the house than he originally thought. There wasn't going to be any way to get closer. He scanned with his night vision glasses and saw no guards, but there was the periodic flash of light that told him the gate around the house had motion sensors. There were probably also ground sensors.

Staying in the woods, he made his way halfway down to the river. He confirmed that the power boat he had seen the man in was still docked. Climbing back to the top, he saw the golf cart. It would appear the man was still at the house, or he had left by some other means. There was only one way to find out.

Dmitri climbed one of the trees closest to the cut area where he could see the entrances to the house and then he waited.

Several hours later, his joints aching, Dmitri considered going home while it was still dawning.

No, I've been here this long, something will surely happen after daybreak, other than me having a harder time getting away.

Shortly after 7am the door opened, and the big man from the park stepped outside. Dmitri felt a sigh of relief. *But where is he going this early?*

A couple of black SUVs pulled up. Dimitri couldn't see the licenses so he didn't know if they were the ones from yesterday. He hadn't put explosives on them, but he would next time, and the state security men would be careless. *Too bad about that.*

Several men got out of the SUVs, and Dmitri recognized them from the day before. *That's a good sign.*

Then he turned back to the door, and another man followed the first one out.

Well now, that's a surprise.

———

THE GROUP WAS SITTING IN THE PANORAMA BAR AFTER HAVING eaten breakfast. They were a little anxious.

"I guess we just take a cab to the Church of Saint John Chrysostom?" asked Jamal.

"We could or maybe Dimitri will drive," replied Dee.

"You really think we're going to hear from him?" asked Mike. "I mean, anything could have happened. His body could be floating down the Volga if they figured out that was him yesterday."

"If we don't hear from him by noon, we'll go on," said Dee. "The ship is scheduled to depart for Uglich this evening."

Dee looked toward Gina, Angelic, and Keno. "I think it might be safer if you all stayed here," he said.

"I don't disagree, at least until we know more, but what if you guys need help?" said Angelic.

"How big is the church?" asked Gina.

"What shape are the murals in?" asked Keno

"Good questions. At least until we hear from Dimitri, we should sit tight."

"I'm getting a little nervous," said Jamal.

A few moments later Dee's phone beeped. The text read, "I'm on the dock."

Dee held up a hand to the others. "I'll be right back."

He reappeared a few moments later with Dimitri in tow. Dimitri nodded at them all. They noticed he looked tired and his khaki suit was more badly rumpled than when they had seen him yesterday.

"Have a seat," said Jamal.

"Thanks," replied Dmitri, collapsing heavily in one of the chairs.

Keno couldn't contain herself. "You look tired," she said.

"I am. I was in a tree outside the dacha for five hours. I'm not as young as I used to be."

"Were you wearing that suit?" asked Gina.

Dimitri smiled. "No, I changed before coming here. This is what I wear when I'm working for myself. It's so plain that people notice it and not me." He raised an arm, sniffed, and then attempted to smooth out some wrinkles. "I suppose I could use another one. I've been living in rural Russia for too long."

"What did you find or what do you think?" asked Dee.

"It was boring until it wasn't. The big guy came out about 7am. His men from yesterday showed up in the SUVs, and then there was a surprise."

"Exciting?" said Gina.

"Yes, I think it confirms that you are definitely on to something or someone thinks you are. Do you remember the man I mentioned yesterday who stabbed my father?"

"Of course," replied Jamal. "You said he is now the head of one of the security agencies."

"True, but he came out the door after the first man. He's

older now himself, but no mistaking him. He's on the hunt for the egg or its secret, if there is one."

"That means this is not state business, but personal," said Dee.

"Mostly," replied Dimitri, "It would depend on how things play out. But, it probably means it's more dangerous for your group. If there is any sort of problem, he'll just dispose of you all. No questions and claim 'state security'."

"The ship leaves this evening. We'd better check the church. What do you suggest?" asked Dee.

"I drove, but let's take a cab. There are many of them, and they are more difficult to tell apart and to follow," said Dimitri. "Any idea what we're looking for?"

"Not really, we didn't even have the right church," replied Jamal.

"You would have figured it out. But what I can't figure is what prompted them to jump you yesterday," said Dimitri.

"Could we be close to something?" asked Dee.

"Let's go see," replied Dimitri.

———

THEY EXITED THE CAB IN FRONT OF THE CHURCH OF SAINT John Chrysostom. The four of them, Dee, Jamal, Mike, and Dimitri, started for the front entrance when Dimitri held up a hand.

"What's different about this church?" asked Dimitri.

They all stopped. "Well, it's similar in size and design to the other churches, except the Alexander Chapel. But like the chapel, this one is predominantly brick, which the others weren't. And what are those shiny surfaces?"

"It's decorated with glazed ceramic tile, inside and out. That is not a feature of the earlier churches. It has extensive artwork inside, much of which is not in good shape. The tile separates some of the murals and defines the interior," said Dee.

Dimitri turned to him.

"It was in the guidebook. I looked it up once you identified the church," replied Dee.

"Let's go have a look," said Mike.

They stepped up into the cupola and inside the main entrance. Looking around briefly, they huddled together.

"The murals are extensive," said Mike.

"And not in good shape," added Jamal.

"It's a good thing we have all afternoon. Even though we may have caught a break in that the main chapel isn't that large, the grounds and surrounding buildings make it look extensive," said Dee.

"What are we looking for?" asked Dimitri while rubbing his eyes.

"Look for a gold door on a room or a building with a church in the next panel beside or around it," replied Dee.

They split up, one in each direction. Many of the murals were badly faded and almost indecipherable along the edges. The scenes were primarily biblical which helped the men eliminate them. They moved slowly, taking it all in but trying to hurry.

Mike came striding over to Dee. "Come and look at this."

"You're sure?"

"Pretty much."

"Let's grab Jamal and Dimitri."

The four of them approached the corner Mike had identified. There was a room with a door in the mural. There was no indication of a building, just the room. The walls of the room were made up of the glazed ceramic tiles in a bright gold color in slightly different patterns on each wall. In the panel beside the room, there was another church.

"Take some pictures Jamal," said Dee.

"What's with the gold tile?" said Mike.

"Does it mean something or is it just part of the building material of this church?" asked Dimitri.

"Has anyone seen any of the tiles in any other murals?" asked Dee.

Everyone shook their heads.

"I got the pictures," said Jamal.

"Let's look for tile in any of the other murals on our way out," said Dee.

They headed for the door but saw nothing else along the way. Back in the cab they started to talk but Dimitri held a finger up to his lips. Silence ensued.

———

THEY GATHERED AGAIN IN THE PANORAMA BAR.

"I didn't want to speak in the cab. The drivers all have ears. We don't need to give anything away. Did you ladies see or hear anything while we were gone?" asked Dimitri.

"We stayed here in the bar mostly or sat in Jamal and Angelic's room. We wanted to be together," replied Gina.

"That was a good idea," replied Dimitri.

"What are you thinking?" asked Jamal.

"Just that I'm surprised those men didn't come after us in the church or try to take the women hostage," replied Dimitri. "But there might be a new strategy with the man I saw today."

"The one from the boat?" asked Keno.

"Yes, he didn't get to be a head of security without being clever. It would have been difficult to snatch or grab either of our groups today, as public as we were. I think he's taken over personally and is content to just watch and see where we lead him. That's the only explanation. The other question is does he know if I'm involved or who I am?"

"How would he know that?" asked Dee. "He didn't see you

this morning and the men yesterday didn't get a good look at you either."

"It would be through surveillance, a tail on the cab, a traffic camera, a talky cabbie, could have been anywhere. For the moment I'll presume he hasn't seen me or know who I am, but I'll need to be more careful."

"Wouldn't he know you from the pursuit of your father and grandfather?" asked Gina.

"It's possible but I don't know that he ever knew I existed. The records would have shown my dead half-brother and sisters. I doubt they knew about me from so late in my father's life."

"What about your name?" asked Keno.

"Kuznetsov is a very common Russian name."

"Still you should be extra careful," said Dee." How will you travel to keep up with us?"

"I'll take a few days off, tell them I'm touring the Golden Circle. Uglich is only a couple of hours by car. I'll be there before you are."

"That reminds me," said Jamal. "We were theorizing whether the 'Golden Circle' could have anything to do with all this? Could it be related to the room or the egg or any of it?"

Dimitri was silent for a moment. "I don't think so. The 'Golden Circle' didn't become a thing until the last few decades when some professor at the Moscow University defined the group of cities and the churches in that circle. He gave it the name."

"So not per se, but maybe, if one of the churches turns out to have a clue."

"Yeah, that's possible, but what is the next church and where is it located. My feeling is that it's leading toward Moscow. And what about the tile in the mural? First time right? What could that possibly mean?"

"Something about the room is all I can imagine," replied Dee. "Since we didn't see any other murals with the tile."

"I just can't figure," said Jamal, "Maybe it isn't relevant and just what the craftsmen the czar sent had to work with."

"Or maybe it was some kind of message to whomever the czar thought might be following the trail," added Mike.

"That's an interesting possibility," said Dimitri. "You can see why I've struggled so many years with it. There are so many variables and so little facts."

"What is the next church?" asked Angelic.

Jamal pulled out his phone and found the picture. Dee pulled out his book and got ready to research.

"It's got five onion domes with a separate bell tower, multi-colored exterior," said Jamal. "There's a peculiar-looking dome on the bell tower and maybe a clock face."

"Well, in Uglich, that looks like it would be the Transformation Cathedral," replied Dee.

"The five, plus or minus, onion domes and the bell tower is a pretty common theme. Most of the churches you've looked at have been some variation of that," said Dimitri.

"Maybe that's also some kind of clue," added Jamal.

"I don't know," said Mike.

"The last two were different," said Gina.

"That little one was creepy," added Keno.

"We'll be there tomorrow, we'll just have to look," said Dee. "Where are you going to stay?" he asked Dimitri.

"The Hotel Moskva," said Dimitri. "It's right above your dock."

"How'd you know that?" asked Gina.

"Being in Naval intelligence is good for some things," replied Dimitri. "I'll be on my way and maybe scout out the church location. There's a closer one to where you will dock, 'Church of Dimitry on the Blood.' But it doesn't have the correct configuration."

Dimitri got up from the table and nodded all around. "I will see you all there. Keep your eyes open in case I'm wrong about the security men. Stick together as much as possible, even on the ship."

———

THEY ATE DINNER THAT NIGHT IN THE FORMAL DINING ROOM and then retired to Dee and Gina's room.

"We'll be leaving shortly but it's not far, a couple of hours and we'll dock in Uglich," said Dee.

"I hope we can find something," added Jamal. "We're going to be in Moscow shortly and out of churches and clues."

"We don't really know that do we?" asked Mike.

"Well, the tour is over and we'll have to move on. I don't think I want to hang around Moscow if state security is looking for us," said Keno.

"She's got a point," added Angelic.

"Surely we can tourist for a day or two. We had that option when we signed up for the cruise, didn't we?" asked Gina.

"That's a good thought," replied Dee. "Why don't you see if you can sign us all up for a couple of extra days or whatever they offer."

"I guess we should get some rest, in case tomorrow is eventful," said Jamal.

13

———

DEE & FRIENDS - DAY 5

Having slept for a few hours, Dee felt the ship turn and then softly bump against the dock. They had arrived in Uglich. He turned to Gina, but she was sleeping soundly.

Dee got up and went to the cabin porthole. Their stateroom was on the port side of the ship and he could look up the bank and see a building. A lighted sign indicated that it was the 'Hotel Moskva'. Dee went back to bed hoping that Dimitri had made it safely.

———

DIMITRI CHECKED IN WITH HIS OFFICE AND TOLD THEM HE WAS taking a few days to tour the Golden Circle, or Golden Ring, of the ancient Russian Orthodox churches. Fortunately Yaroslavl, where he was located, was on the circle but Uglich was not. Dimitri waited until late in the day, in case someone was following him, before leaving so that he had a plausible excuse for driving the few hours to Uglich, rather than continuing on around the Circle.

It was late, and there wasn't much traffic. Dimitri watched closely for a tail, and while he didn't spot one, he couldn't shake the feeling that someone was back there. Pulling into the hotel's parking lot, he made a note of all the vehicles that were present, went inside, checked in, and went to bed.

The following morning on his way to the car, supposedly to drive for some breakfast, he saw what looked like a state sedan, which hadn't been there the night before. *It would have been nice if it had been one of the SUVs, then I'd know.* He looked down to the river and saw that the longship had docked during the night. There was little activity on deck. He drove a short distance, ate breakfast, and returned. The sedan hadn't moved. *Either it's just coincidence or they knew I wasn't leaving, if they are here for me. Maybe they are just following the ship.*

Dimitri texted Dee. "How long before the tour begins?"

Dee responded, "Shortly."

Dimitri replied, "We'll meet afterwards, enjoy the sights, there should be a lot to see."

Dee sent him a 'thumbs up.'

Fortunately for Dimitri, his room overlooked the parking lot, and he could sit by the window and watch both his own vehicle and the state sedan.

As the tour group offloaded from the longship and boarded the bus, Dimitri saw two men he hadn't seen before exit the hotel and approach the sedan. As they did so one of them went over to Dimitri's vehicle and put his hand on the hood. *No doubt it's still warm since I just returned.* Then the man dropped out of sight beside the car. *That's not good. They've made me as an accomplice. The car is useless now. I brought in everything with me. No need to go back. Do they know who I am? It doesn't really matter. I'm just another obstacle now.*

Dimitri watched the man return to the sedan and climb inside. The car pulled out after the tour bus rolled away.

Dimitri gathered everything but his extra clothes and hustled out of the room, heading downstairs to catch a cab.

——————

THEY BOARDED THE BUS AND AFTER A SHORT TOUR AROUND downtown and a quick walk through the central district; they headed for the Transfiguration Cathedral, the most prominent church in Uglich.

It was a grand multi-story building with murals from bottom to top. They ditched the tour and assembled near the altar.

"Everybody knows what to look for. The scenes have been in obscure locations so far. Just keep your eyes open and text if you see something," said Dee.

They broke up and started out in different directions. There was a consistency in size of large groups of the murals, which made them easier to scan. For the most part they were separated by gold covered columns and gilt, which also made it easier to scan and move along.

Forty-five minutes passed, and no one had anything to report. They had covered large portions of the cathedral.

Jamal ran into Dee as they circled the walls. "Maybe we hit a dead end this time? Maybe this isn't the right church."

"Maybe. But that bell tower was distinctive, unless there's another one like it somewhere."

"What do you think happened with Dimitri?"

"I don't know. He must have been checking something. Apparently he trusts us enough to locate the clue, if there is one."

"You don't suppose it's trouble do you? I mean, I'd think he'd want to be here."

"Maybe he got another lead?"

"What could it be?"

"We know so little, it's hard to tell."

They saw Keno approaching. She waved at them. "Come and see this."

"Should we get the others?" asked Dee.

"Take a look first."

Dee and Jamal followed her to another corner of the church. It was a wall between two doorways that led to the back of the church.

They both stood still and stared for a moment. There were three murals, side by side. The first was the room with the golden door. Interior walls were visible, and they were colored bright gold with different textures on each wall.

"Those textures have to mean something," said Jamal.

"I agree, but what?" replied Dee.

"This is it?" asked Keno.

"Yes, you did good. Do you want to go get the others?" asked Dee.

Keno smiled at them and hustled off.

Jamal had his camera out and was taking pictures. "What does it mean?" he asked.

"This is the clearest depiction yet. The room is in the first panel, the Winter Palace showing the door is in the second panel, and the third panel leads us to a church."

"We should be able to identify this one," said Jamal.

"I already have. It's Saint Basil's Cathedral in Red Square in Moscow. It's the most famous cathedral in Russia. There are eleven different churches inside. Look for something that might tell us which one."

"Oh, really?" said Jamal.

"Yeah, needle in a haystack compared to what we've been searching for."

The others arrived with a breathless Keno in front.

"What did you find?" asked Angelic.

Gina pointed. "Is that it?"

"St. Basil's in Moscow. One of our last stops on the tour."

"What do you think we'll find?" asked Mike.

"Hopefully something that pulls this all together."

DIMITRI ELECTED NOT TO FOLLOW THE TOUR BUS, HOPING THAT the security men were only along to observe and not secure his new friends. Instead, he went straight to the Transfiguration Cathedral. From his vantage point, he had seen the group scouring around looking but had kept himself invisible as he had not seen the security men and didn't want to give himself away.

Dimitri saw Dee and the group headed for the door and decided they must have found whatever there was to find. He wanted to join them but still hadn't seen the security men. He maintained his position and kept watching. After seeing Dee and the others rejoin the tour and head for the exit, Dimitri saw the two men from the sedan appear. They glanced about as well. *Probably looking for me.*

He remained hidden until the men turned and exited as well. He stayed for several minutes and then deposited himself in the middle of the next large crowd of people exiting the building. Once outside, he scoured the parking lot for signs of the security men's sedan. Satisfied that he didn't see it, Dimitri hailed a cab and returned to the hotel.

Several hours later Dimitri received a text from Dee. It read, "We're here."

He had been watching the parking lot for some time and had not seen the sedan return. He estimated they wouldn't want to be around if or when his car exploded. But they, or someone, was probably watching.

Arriving back at the longship, Dee texted Dimitri. He and the others cleaned up quickly and met in the Panorama Bar. Dee had not heard back from Dimitri, and while they waited they discussed the day and dinner.

"I don't understand why we're going to the big church in Moscow if the gold room is in St. Petersburg," said Jamal.

"It doesn't seem to make a lot of sense, unless something in St Basil's tells us where to look in the Winter Palace. I mean the whole thing, the room, could have been gone long ago, destroyed by the Soviets."

"Yeah, and what part did the pearl play in any of this?" added Mike.

"You'd better figure it out soon," said Angelic, "The trip's almost over."

"Oh, I did get us an extended stay in Moscow for three extra days," said Gina.

"Really?" asked Keno. Gina nodded at her. "But, if the room is back in St. Petersburg, what are we going to do? How will we get there?" asked Keno.

"I don't know. We still have too many unanswered questions," replied Dee.

They turned at the sound of someone approaching, and Dimitri appeared before them.

"Have a seat," said Jamal.

Dimitri dropped in between Angelic and Gina. "Hello," he said.

"You still look tired," said Keno.

"Yes, I'm afraid I am. My news is not good." He glanced around the table.

"Please continue," said Dee.

"I apparently was followed from Yaroslavl although I never saw anyone. This morning there was a state car in the lot that wasn't there the night before. Two men went out and got in it and followed your tour group. Before they left, they went to my car and planted something, probably a car bomb. I stayed away from it."

"How did they find you?" asked Mike.

"Someone must have identified me at the park on the river. Anyway, I took a cab to the Transformation Church, and I saw you there. It appears you had some success. I also saw the security men follow you out. Have you seen anything?"

Most of them shook their heads.

"That's good. I was concerned to come over here in case someone was assigned to watch and see if my car blew up. But then if they already were aware of me and certainly of you, I came ahead. I'm still guessing they have decided to watch us and see what happens. Please keep that in mind. So, what did you find?"

"It was the first three panel scene. The room in one, the Winter Palace in the second, and St Basil's in Moscow in the third," said Jamal.

"Any ideas what it means?" asked Dimitri.

"The walls in the room scene were textured again. That has to mean something. We just don't know what," added Dee.

"St Basil's has eleven different sanctuaries, churches actually, inside," said Dimitri.

"We figured that," replied Dee.

"We're still looking at the photographs," said Jamal, pulling out his phone. "To see if there's any type of clue which one or where to start."

"We have managed to stay a couple of extra days in Moscow," added Gina.

"Normally I'd say that was good, but with security on all of us now, I don't know," replied Dimitri.

"I thought you said they were just watching us and waiting," said Dee.

"I think that's true right now, but it might change at any time." Dimitri paused for a moment. "My grandfather's last post was an administrative one at St. Basil's. He was quite old. His wife had died. My father thought they just made a spot for him. He offered my grandfather the opportunity to come and live with him. But this was the mid-1950s, and it would have been difficult for an old man to defect or escape. Church officials found him slumped over his desk. No autopsy was performed, which always made my father suspicious."

"What would he have done with the pearl by that time?" asked Keno.

"That's a good question. My father and I always thought he would have left it, hidden, at the church where Anastasia gave it to him. But I've been all over that church, and it appeared that others had as well."

"So if they found it, there's more to the puzzle?" asked Dee.

"I don't think they found it or it would be on display with the other one. Sergei Dimitrov spent his whole life looking for the pearl."

"Maybe his assistant found it later," said Gina. "Would he have kept it?"

"Perhaps, if he thought it might lead to something more. But otherwise he would have turned it over to the state. That pearl would be hard to sell, even on the black market. Fabergé only made those two. If he sold it and word got out, the Soviets would have killed him and all his family slowly and painfully."

"So you don't think the egg has been found?" said Jamal.

"That's my feeling or best guess."

"Could there be other churches?" asked Angelic. "Where your grandfather was located."

"I think he was mostly at the church in St. Petersburg until he got really old."

"Are there other churches near that one where your grandfather was?" asked Gina. "Like there were a couple of clues in Yaroslavl."

"Yeah," added Keno. "There's a church right here beside us that's not far from Transformation, could there be other clues?"

"I suppose it's possible. But the one here next to us is the Church of Dimitry on the Blood. It was the site where Ivan the Terrible's son, Dimitry, was killed. Ivan was the first Czar of Russia in 1547, but he ended up being the last ruler of the Rurik Dynasty, which had governed for four hundred years. Ivan's son was just a young boy, and at Ivan's death one of the members of his court killed the boy, right over there where the church is located. It was built in the son's honor by the Romanoffs but they would have nothing to do with it in terms of their own family secrets. They ascended to the throne about fifteen years after Ivan was killed, during what the Russians call 'the time of troubles', and they ruled for the next four hundred years. By the early 20th century they were interrelated to every other royal family in Europe."

"But you said none of them came to the Romanoffs' aid when the Bolsheviks took over," said Angelic.

"That's right," replied Dimitri. "I guess they weren't that close. King George V of England thought about it, he and Nicholas were 1st cousins, but the king decided it wasn't politically expedient."

"That would have altered all of Europe, World War II, and the Cold War," said Mike.

"Yeah, probably. I think it certainly would have been different than it was."

"But, back to now. What do we do?" asked Dee.

"I think you go on with the tour."

"What are you going to do?" asked Jamal.

Dimitri grinned. "I've already done it. The ship had an extra berth, and I signed on for the last leg of the tour."

Jamal stuck out his hand. "Welcome aboard."

14

DEE & FRIENDS - DOWN THE RIVER

They departed Uglich the next morning. During the night Dee heard an explosion and got up to look out the port side. There was a fire in the hotel parking lot.

Gina looked over at him. "Car thief, I suppose," replied Dee. "Dimitri is on board with us."

They met the next morning for breakfast. Afterwards Dee asked, "Did you hear that explosion last night?"

Dimitri grinned. "I did. I hope it wasn't an innocent. Probably a thief since the car hadn't moved for a couple of days, and it was the middle of the night."

"What will security think?" asked Jamal.

"With any luck, if there was a body, they might think it was me trying to sneak away. Then I might have a little time before they identify the remains."

"It's nice outside. Let's go up on the deck and sightsee," said Gina.

"It would be fun," added Angelic.

"Please," said Keno.

They wondered up to the deck and stood at the rail, watching the countryside slip past.

"It's beautiful," said Gina.

"Just don't be here in the winter," replied Dimitri.

"Look there's something in the water up ahead," called Keno.

Dimitri didn't look. "I expect it's the Kalyazin Bell Tower. This lake, actually the Uglich Reservoir, was created by Stalin in the 1930s for hydro power. He flooded several small villages. Kalyazin is also the name of the remaining town. Portions of it were submerged, including the Monastery of Saint Nicholas. The bell tower is the only thing that survived. I remember my father telling me my grandfather was there for a time." It was like a realization hit him and Dimitri turned to gaze at the tower. "I guess my grandfather was in some other places besides St Petersburg and Moscow. Which means our task could have just gotten exponentially harder. The pearl could be anywhere."

"It looks abandoned," said Mike. "Although there is a small dock adjacent to it. Just enough for a small boat to tie off on."

"Curiosity seekers no doubt," said Dimitri. He gazed at it again. "I remember my father saying that my grandfather said the bell in the tower was commissioned in 1895 as a commemorative of Nicholas II's coronation." He stood staring again. "Maybe I've been going about the search for the pearl all wrong."

"Why's that?" asked Jamal.

"I've always looked at it as where would my grandfather hide it. The church? The area around it? Would he have kept it with him, especially after Sergei Dimitrov began pursuing it and him? Where would he hide it?"

"You said your father thought your grandfather held it thinking he would give it back to the Romanoffs. That to him would have been Nicholas II. Could the hiding place have something to do with the czar?"

"Exactly," replied Dimitri. "St Basil's in Moscow. Eleven sanctuaries and churches, probably a thousand good hiding places. Maybe we're on to something."

"Do you think the murals might tell us or will there be murals?" asked Jamal.

"There really hasn't been any clues about anything hidden, just the gold texture on the walls and the fact that it looks like an entire room," replied Dee.

———

THEY WERE WAY PAST THE BELL TOWER NOW AND LEANING INTO the breeze, looking back, considering what they had just talked about. Dimitri was at one end of the group.

"Look," said Keno. "Islands, more areas that didn't flood."

Everyone turned to look and there was a loud boom, like a car backfiring or a firecracker. Then there was the sound of a ricochet off the metal of the boat housing.

"Get down everybody!" screamed Dimitri. "We're under fire."

They lay on the deck for several minutes until they were well past the island.

"Everyone stay down," said Dimitri. "I think that shot was for me. I was at the back of the group. They want you alive but they're tired of me being around and have decided that I'm not important to them."

He slid down the side of the boat a few feet and scanned the islands behind them. "Slip down the hatchway one at a time."

———

THEY MET AGAIN IN THE PANORAMA BAR.

"I'm sorry that happened," said Dimitri. "They clearly don't want or need me to be around. I think they are watching you until they see something. You're probably safe until then, or maybe not."

"How do they know it's you?" asked Dee.

"I don't know, maybe they don't? I'm just not part of your group, and they resent the addition. Or maybe they've seen me or, maybe my cover's blown, after all these years. I'm not high ranking or important as I said. They mostly just leave me alone, on both sides. I'm a relic from the Cold War."

"What do we do?" asked Angelic.

"I need to lie low and not be seen as part of your group," replied Dimitri. "I don't want to endanger you. We'll be in Moscow soon so hopefully we'll find an answer at St. Basil's."

"You saved Dee and me at Yaroslavl Park. How can we help you?" asked Jamal.

"I think I just need to stay out of sight until you find the next clue," said Dimitri. "It's probably safest if the women stay on board when you go into St. Basil's, in case they move on you. I can look after the women while they are on board. When you're touring other parts of Red Square, go as a group, be tourists. Keep them guessing."

"Won't they be suspicious if just the men come out? How about the men slip away while the women are shopping, confuse the issue?" asked Mike.

"That could work. It depends on how effective you are at giving them the slip. There are eyes everywhere. People are afraid not to cooperate," said Dimitri. "It's only about four hours to Moscow from here. We'll dock tonight and they'll begin excursions in the morning. Take the Red Square one, get a look around. I'll stay on the longship and out of sight."

15

DEE & FRIENDS - RED SQUARE BOUND

They met with Dimitri in the morning for breakfast.

"Look, there are many things to see in Red Square. St. Basil's is at one end. They'll drop you off at the Resurrection Gate on the other end, between the Moscow city hall and the State Historical Museum. There's the Kazan Cathedral, the GUM Store, the tomb of Lenin, and the Kremlin, which has the Senate building, several palaces, some churches, and other government buildings behind the walls. The Spasskaya Tower is on the eastern wall of the Kremlin. It's the building with the red star on top. St. Basil's is at the far end. The GUM store runs almost the length of the square."

"Is it called Red Square for the Communists?" asked Keno. "Like the Red Star?"

"No to the Square, but yes to the star. The Communists put the star up in the mid-1930s to replace the double-headed eagle, which was one of the last remaining symbols of the czars. In the early Russian language, 'Krasnaya Ploschad', which is what the area was called, translates roughly to 'Red Square.' It probably had to do with the brick streets or the majority of the buildings in red brick."

"Convenient for the Communists," said Angelic.

"Yeah, they liked the name, and it stuck."

"The GUM Store isn't red brick," said Jamal.

"It was built in the 1800s, later than most of the other buildings. It was originally a trading center, with many small shops and stores, but then the Communists turned it into an office building in the 1930s, but back to retail in the 1950s."

"Most of the churches weren't churches either," said Dee.

"The Bolsheviks didn't believe in organized religion. They left a few of the churches functional, but converted many to museums or mixed use of some kind. It wasn't until the 1980s and 1990s that many of them were given back to the church and restoration efforts began."

"It's amazing they survived," said Dee.

"The people still respected the structure and protected it unless the Bolsheviks took a particular interest in one and destroyed or defaced it."

He continued. "See what you can see about the layout of the Square and how you might best enter St. Basil's. When you want to come back, I can get you around on the subway system. It's the second largest in the world and by far the most ornate and elaborate. You probably won't find anything inexpensive in the GUM store, but there are booths and shops about the Square that may sell more traditional and cheaper Russian or local looking clothing. Pick some up if you see them. When we go on the subway and back to the church, you won't stand out as much as a tourist. Your clothing is very western."

"I thought Russians liked western clothing, western things," said Keno.

"They do, but they're not always accessible or affordable to all Russians."

"That's why your khaki suit worked so well," said Jamal.

Dimitri grinned at him. "Exactly, Russian clothing makes you invisible."

———

WE ASSEMBLED AND TOOK THE BUSES THROUGH THE CITY. After a quick tour, we departed at the Resurrection Gate at the northwestern end of Red Square.

"I'm glad Dimitri told us what to look for," said Jamal.

"It might help us find our way more quickly and see what's possible for slipping away to St. Basil's," added Mike.

"The GUM store is right across the walkway from St. Basil's," said Dee. "That's probably our best chance."

"The tour is supposed to take us into St. Basil's. We can get a look around without being obvious. Stay with the group and look like a tourist," said Gina.

"Good plan," replied Dee.

———

THEY FOLLOWED THE TOUR GUIDE AROUND THE SQUARE ON foot, stopping at each of the buildings or structures Dimitri had mentioned plus a few more. The tour was to last most of the day. They broke for lunch.

"There are several restaurants and food tents or trucks around the Square. Meet back here in an hour and we'll visit the GUM store and St. Basil's," said the guide.

"What's for lunch?" asked Mike.

"The guide-book says Italian, Italian, pizza, Russian, and other," said Gina.

"Pizza," said Jamal and Keno at the same time.

"Pizza?" replied Angelic. "We're in Russia, what would they know about pizza?"

"Let's go find out," said Mike.

"The name of the restaurant is the 'Bosco Mishka Bar'," added Gina. "It should be right over there." She pointed to the closest building.

"It's a bar with pizza, and it's not far. Let's go," said Keno.

———

RALLYING BACK WITH THE TOUR GUIDE AFTER A SATISFYING round of pizza and beverages, they prepared for the last half of the tour.

"Pretty good pizza, for Russia," said Jamal.

"It was excellent. When did we have pizza last?" asked Mike.

"Don't remember, Mexico or Spain," added Dee.

———

"WE'LL TOUR THE BASICS OF THE GUM STORE BUT NOT HAVE much time for shopping," said the guide. "If you see something and can purchase it quickly, go for it, but we'll bring you back tomorrow with more time to look and buy."

"That could be our opportunity," whispered Jamal to Dee.

"We'll see if that works for Dimitri," replied Dee.

After a quick stop in the GUM store, which was 800 feet long per the guide, the group moved on to St. Basil's.

They stopped at the entrance of the church. "Let's take a moment for a brief history before we go inside," said the guide. "The structure is called St. Basil's. It was originally called the 'Trinity Church.' There are eleven churches under nine differently colored domes. Under each of them is a different church or chapel. All of which surround a central chapel dedicated to the Virgin Mary. The other chapels are:

Chapel of the Three Patriarchs

Chapel of St. Nicholas

Church of John the Blessed
Chapel of the Holy Martyrs Cyprian and Justina
Chapel of the Holy Trinity
Chapel of the Entry of Our Lord
Chapel of St. Alexander of Svir
Church of St. Gregory of Armenia
Chapel of St. Varlaam of Khutyn."
A hand went up in the crowd. "That's only ten."

"Correct," the guide replied, "And there won't be a quiz. But the eleventh one was added when St. Vasily the Blessed, also known as 'Basil', died and was buried on site. The final chapel was named for him. Ivan the Terrible built the original in 1552 to commemorate his victory over the Tartars, which opened the way for Russia to expand into Asia, primarily Siberia."

"That was quite the prize," whispered Jamal.

Dee nodded in return. "Let's be sharp but not suspicious when we get inside."

The guide continued. "The church is now primarily a museum and part of the State Historical Museum system. However, services are held on occasion in some of the chapels. Stay close together as there are dark and winding passages between the chapels and the exhibits. We won't be going downstairs as it is a very dark and less visited area. There are murals wall to wall and floor to ceiling in most of the chapels. There are thousands of them in a variety of sizes. You could spend a week and not see them all. As I said, stay together, it's quite dark in places. It's a labyrinth and easy to get lost."

The group followed the guide up the steps and through the main entrance in a tight throng. It was a well-lit glass enclosed space that looked like a museum. From there they began to wander along behind the guide as she moved from chapel to chapel.

"How many murals do you think there are?" whispered Jamal to Dee.

"She was right, probably thousands if each chapel is like that one. More like stars in the sky, as high as some of them are. We'll never be able to see them all or have the time to examine many of them."

"What can we do?"

"I don't know. Maybe this is where it ends. We can ask Dimitri if he has any thoughts. It seems impossible."

They walked through eight other areas without stopping in any of them. It was one long continuous hike, and they were back at the main entrance.

"All I saw was the magnitude of the place," said Mike as they stood together before leaving the cathedral.

"She was right. I would have been lost in a minute," added Keno.

"You'd have to have a map. The best I could see was this overview of the chapels and not the interior." Gina held up a paper handout for the others to see.

"I don't know how you are going to find anything," said Angelic.

They followed the guide out and across the Square. It was later in the day and darkness was descending as they made their way back to the buses.

Once boarded, the guide turned to them again. "Tomorrow we will return to the GUM Store for those of you who want to shop. There will also be excursions into other parts of the city. They'll make the announcements at dinner tonight or on the website."

They rode the rest of the way in silence.

16

DEE & FRIENDS - WHAT'S NEXT

Back on the longship, they cleaned up and gathered for dinner.

"So what did you think of Red Square?" asked Dimitri.

"It's impressive in its size and age," said Angelic.

"That GUM Store was amazing, one of the biggest retail centers I've ever seen," added Keno.

"Everything was made of red brick, except the store," said Gina.

"The inside of the church was unbelievable," added Jamal.

"You got any thoughts on that?" asked Dee.

"Such as?" replied Dimitri.

"Even if we can get in there, how are we going to be able to find anything? There are murals everywhere. Many of them are high up on the walls. We've had that in the past but there weren't so many of them," answered Dee. "It's overwhelming."

"Yeah, I feared that. You've been lucky so far in finding the clues, although I'm not sure how much they've told you. We still don't really know what they mean or what you're looking for."

"You're after the egg. We haven't seen anything about that."

"Yes, I've continued thinking about it. As I said, maybe I've gone about it wrong all these years. I've always thought my grandfather hid the egg somewhere and planned to retrieve it when the time was right. What if he kept it closer to him, to keep an eye on it? My father told me, and I saw it with my own eyes when they killed him, Sergei and his men were always looking for the egg."

"If they thought your grandfather had it why didn't they just grab him and torture him until he told them?" asked Jamal.

"I've never been quite sure of that. Maybe because him having it was just a rumor or maybe his age or faith made them feel like he might never tell them."

"Was his faith that strong?" asked Dee.

"I couldn't really answer that. My grandfather was a strong-willed man, but they are masters at punishment and torture. I think it's more likely they weren't sure he had it and preferred to watch him over time, maybe he'd slip up and give away its location. He always said that Sergei was the only one looking, and the rest of the Bolsheviks thought the royal family had probably hidden it somewhere or destroyed it. That maybe one day it would turn up. It would have been hard to disguise and probably ended up in one of the politburos' private collections anyway."

"Going back to what you were thinking," said Gina, "do you have a new idea on where the egg might be located?"

"Yes. It occurred to me that grandfather might have moved the egg around with him to keep it safe. My dad told me that Grandfather told him on several occasions that his house or apartment had been searched and that he had been searched and beaten while being questioned by Sergei. I always had in mind that Grandfather spent most of his career at the church outside St. Petersburg, but then when we were sailing into Moscow and passed the sunken monastery and then looking at St. Basil's, I remembered he had moved around several times later in his career. The last place was St. Basil's."

"So you think maybe he had it there?" asked Dee.

"I think it's possible. I searched the church in St. Petersburg multiple times. But so did Sergei. Of course, anyone could have found it over time and hid it away somewhere totally different. Or it could have been at the monastery and is beneath the waters of the reservoir. The possibilities are endless."

"But there's nothing your father ever told you?" asked Jamal.

"No. I've replayed the conversations we had over and over in my head. My father felt like my grandfather never told him in order to protect him. And when I saw Sergei kill my father, I think Dad would probably have told him if he knew anything."

"Your father didn't believe as strongly as your grandfather?" asked Angelic.

"I think his beliefs and character were as strong, but he had a fondness for the czar and his family, but so much had happened and the Romanoffs were never coming back, Dad would have told them, just to end the struggle."

"That makes sense," added Mike. "But what about the guy that was with Sergei? You say he's still looking for the egg?"

"He appears to be. I don't know what Sergei told him. For Sergei it was personal. I mean I heard the stories, years later after Sergei was high ranking, about how he had been questioned about the egg and the dagger. But he survived and prospered. But the taint remained at least until he died."

"That was just part of their political process, wasn't it?" asked Angelic.

"A part of it. The Bolsheviks were very competitive and

ruthless. Anything to create an advantage, which is why I think Sergei never stopped looking for the egg."

"But he never gave up the dagger," said Gina.

"I think he saw that as a symbol of power. His tie to the old regime and his strength in the new one. It was a weapon of war, even as highly stylized as it was. It didn't have near the prestige of the egg, although it was quite valuable. Finding the egg would have made him a hero."

"Turning the egg in might have been seen as him relinquishing something he had hidden for all those years. Maybe used against him?" added Keno.

"That's very possible but I think he was willing to take that risk."

"So, again, you had a different thought about your grandfather and the egg?" asked Dee.

"Yes. He died, or was killed, in St. Basil's. Dad offered him the opportunity to come and live with us, but he wouldn't take it. I think it was because of the egg. He could never have gotten it out, and he wouldn't leave it behind. I think he had it close to him. And as you said, St. Basil's is huge, a thousand places to hide things. My suspicion is that Sergei did finally kill him, there in the basement of St. Basil's."

"In the basement?" asked Dee.

"Yes, that's where the staff's quarters were in those days. I think it's just minor exhibits and storage these days."

"We didn't go down there," said Keno. "The guide said it was dark, full of shadows, and rarely visited."

"That might be the place to look for the egg," said Dee.

"We could split up and some of us look for the mural while others look for the egg," added Jamal.

"That's probably not a good idea," replied Dimitri.

"Why not?" asked Angelic.

"It is dark and dangerous, and we don't know if we can give them the slip," replied Dimitri.

"We didn't see anyone today," said Gina. "I kept asking Dee if he thought anyone was watching us."

"From certain points on the Square they could watch you without ever moving or being seen. That is one of the most surveilled areas in the world. They saw you."

"Did you see anything here?" asked Keno.

"I never went on deck, but I took a couple of peeks from the Panorama Bar. There were a number of State vehicles in the parking lot. The dock area is another highly monitored spot."

"What do we do?" asked Dee.

"I think the women can best serve as a diversion. Separating them from the men will come closer to keeping them safe. You do realize if we go poking around in the church and are caught, you'll never get out of this country alive?"

There were brief glances among the group. "How will you go with us?" asked Jamal.

"A disguise," replied Dimitri. "If I can borrow some of your clothing, I'll dress up as a tourist and blend in with your group. A baseball cap and a gaudy shirt, maybe a camera around my neck, should do the trick."

"I've got a pair of Levis you can borrow," said Jamal.

"That should work," replied Dimitri, "very western and highly coveted in Russia."

He continued. "I suggest we let the women go shopping alone tomorrow, to plant the idea of doing things separately. So they won't be too alarmed if we're not all together. The rest of us can stay on the ship and plan. We'll consider when and where to look inside the church. Hopefully, we can find some strong flashlights and comfortable clothes." He turned to the women. "Among the many other things you buy tomorrow try to locate small powerful flashlights, batteries, and dark comfortable clothing for each of the men. Not all black, just darker rather than brighter. We don't want to seem out of the ordinary when we go out the day after tomorrow. How much longer can we stay on the ship?"

"We have three more days," replied Gina.

"We'll have to act fast. I did some research today while you were gone, and I have floor plan maps of the church, for each level. On your suggestion, we'll concentrate on the basement for the egg. You can decide how you want to pursue the mural."

"Maybe from your floor plans we can decide how to divide it up," said Dee. "Maybe we can filter the search in some way? Has there been anything consistent in the location of the other murals?"

"They were usually somewhat remote," replied Gina.

"Maybe we should start looking in the basement too?" said Jamal.

"Bottom to top?" asked Mike.

"I suppose that's as good as any. We don't have much time," answered Dee.

———

THE FOLLOWING MORNING THEY WATCHED GINA, ANGELIC, AND Keno troop off to the bus for the GUM Store.

"Who knows how much poorer we'll be when they return," said Mike.

"Dimitri did tell them to mix in the purchases for us with ones for themselves," replied Jamal.

"You reckon Dimitri is paying for it?" asked Dee.

"Not on my salary," replied Dimitri. "I never shop in the GUM Store, too expensive and too flashy."

"So, what do you think about how we do this tomorrow?" Dee asked Dimitri.

"We go into the GUM store with the women. We work our

way closest to the church, make our way over to it, and start our search in the basement."

"That simple?" asked Jamal.

"Let's not make it harder than we have to or so rigid that we can't be flexible. That's the biggest thing in the field, be adaptable and have a plan of denial for whatever you're doing."

"Has the interior changed significantly as a museum? Where else could your grandfather have hidden the egg?" asked Dee.

"Could it be up high somewhere? A balcony? Rafters? Was there scaffolding at some point? Some access to the interior domes?" asked Jamal.

"I imagine there were all those things, and he might have used them, less accessible, which might keep them better hidden. But, if he was carrying or moving the egg around with him, I'd think he'd want something easy and quick to get to and not so visible," replied Dimitri.

"So the basement seems better?" asked Dee.

"I think it's the best place to start, but face it, the egg could be anywhere or nowhere."

Dimitri handed each of them a copy of the basement floor plan. "We can go downstairs right after we get inside and start below the main entrance and work our way around."

"How much time do we have?" asked Mike.

"They close at 6pm. We only have one day. We must be quick. We have a very small window, and that's if we don't get interrupted."

THE MEN SPENT THE REST OF THE MORNING AND MUCH OF THE afternoon plotting and planning for their task. The women returned shortly before dinner with many bags. They came into the Panorama Bar carrying all their packages and waving them in the air.

"Look what we got," shouted Keno.

Angelic and Gina waved their bags in the air.

"Let's adjourn and we'll show you our purchases," said Angelic. "Follow me to our stateroom." She led the way to the elevator and down a deck. Everyone followed along.

The women stood together in the living room, and the men sat on the couch and chairs. While Gina and Keno pulled out various outfits and waved them about, Angelic subtly pulled out small handheld flashlights and packs of batteries, which she quickly waved in front of the men and then returned to the bag. After the two women finished pulling out their clothes, they removed pants and shirts which they tossed to each man, dark pants and dark tee shirts.

"Looks like you ladies were successful," said Dimitri.

"We thought so," replied Angelic. "There is a bus in the early morning and one in the late morning headed for Red Square. It's kind of an open session. See what you want with an assigned time for pickup."

"That sounds great," said Dimitri. "Let's take the early one."

There were nods all around.

"Okay then, let's grab some dinner and get an early night. Get plenty of rest. Gentlemen wear something bright over your tee shirt that you can take off and let your spouse carry out. Ladies wear something bright."

17

DEE & FRIENDS - BACK TO THE SQUARE

They met early the next morning and ate a light breakfast while chatting quietly among themselves.

"Ladies, be sure to shop slowly," said Dimitri.

"I think the last bus is 4pm," said Angelic.

"That's correct," replied Dimitri. "And even if we're not back, be sure you are on it. Come back here and stay together."

"How will you get back?" asked Gina.

"Subway, or Metro as they call it here."

"Moscow Metro, cool," said Keno. "I heard they are elaborate, very ornate."

"That is true, although I hope I don't have to show them to these gentlemen."

THEY CAUGHT THE BUS AND RODE IN SILENCE TO THE Resurrection Gate. The bus was not nearly so full as it had been. Many of the cruise passengers had departed. Only those with extended stays remained.

"It would have been nice if the bus were still full," whispered Dimitri to the others. "But they'd find us anyway, so just relax. We are going shopping for the day, decadent westerners."

They trooped off the bus and made their way slowly but steadily toward the GUM Store.

"Let's stay together until we get to the center of the store and then you ladies take a different direction from the men. Remember to stay busy but go slow. Gentlemen, we'll make our way to the far end of the store individually and then decide how to cross to the church. Stroll, but walk steadily, look at something occasionally," said Dimitri.

They followed the plan and Gina, Angelic, and Keno spun off to a different part of the store. They had collected the over shirts of the men at various points as they walked through the aisles, so that the men were now in dark pants and dark shirts. They split up after the women left and several minutes later found themselves in the vicinity of the exit.

Dimitri told each of them, "Look for a group that appears to be headed for the church and follow along with them. When they veer, stay with them as long as you can, jump to another group if possible, or make your way steadily, without running, to the church and go inside. Do not linger."

Mike went first with an elderly group of couples that were headed for the church. Then Jamal followed two young Russian girls who immediately started talking to him. He smiled and followed along.

Dee and Dimitri waited for several minutes and then followed a couple of elderly women out the door, appearing as if to be two couples. The two women looked back at them suspiciously.

"What are you doing?" the first one asked in heavily accented English.

"Just walking along behind," replied Dimitri in Russian and then English.

"Your Russian is good," said the second woman.

"That's because I live here," replied Dimitri.

They kept walking. "Where are you going?" asked the first woman.

"To St. Basil's."

"We are headed to the Spasskaya Tower so we won't be together much longer."

"Enjoy your walk," answered Dimitri, and he and Dee peeled away from the women and fell in behind a group of tourists that were headed for St. Basil's entrance.

"Lucky for us," said Dee.

"Maybe, if those women don't go straight to the nearest authority and turn us in," said Dimitri.

"Why would they do that?"

"Russians don't trust anyone and try to protect themselves by being informants."

"So we may have even less time than we thought?"

"It's possible." They climbed the steps and entered the Cathedral. "You and I will stay together and let Mike and Jamal work together."

Dee nodded as they approached the two men who were standing and waiting by an entrance to the lower level.

"Let's get started," said Dimitri as he led the way down the steps.

Once at the bottom, they found themselves in a short dark hallway with a lighted room just beyond. They entered the room to an exhibit of Russian artifacts.

"Everyone pull out your map," said Dimitri. "We'll start clockwise and move around the basement, chapel by chapel. Use your flashlights in the hallways and corridors. Hopefully, we won't run in to many people. Move as quick as you can.

Dee and I will focus on hiding places for the egg, you two look for the mural. If you get ahead of us, just keep going. If we get separated, meet at the base of the stairs."

Two hours and four chapels later they hadn't seen anything that looked promising. Mike and Jamal were typically finishing an area as Dee and Dimitri moved into it. All four of them were currently under the main chapel located at the center of the cathedral.

"This is the biggest space down here and will just leave us the remaining chapels to review," said Dimitri.

"You said your grandfather was housed down here. Do you know which area, or have we already looked at it?" asked Dee.

Dimitri shook his head before speaking. "These maps weren't old enough to show that, and I never heard my father say."

Mike and Jamal had moved into the next corridor. Dimitri and Dee stood talking for a moment when Mike stuck his head back into the room. "Come see this." And he disappeared back into the hallway.

Dee and Dimitri scurried across the room and down a short corridor. Jamal was standing in front of a painting that covered the wall at the end of the hall.

As they rushed toward it, Dee saw a small brass plaque on the wall. He stopped. It read, "This area of the building was the former location of the living quarters for Cathedral staff."

Dimitri shone a light on it. He turned to Dee and said, "I'm surprised they would memorialize that fact."

Dee shrugged. "At least we know we are in the right area finally." But then he turned to look at the painting.

It was a painting of a man, life-size, in a robe, with a golden aura around his head. His arms were outstretched in each direction and surrounding him along the edges of the wall were smaller paintings of multiple scenes.

"Who does that look like?" asked Jamal.

"Nicholas II," replied Dee.

"Agreed," added Dimitri.

"Isn't this church too old for him, the last czar?" asked Mike.

"Yes," added Dimitri.

"It would have had to have been added later, somewhere around the time of Nicholas," said Dee.

"It's definitely newer," added Jamal. "See how much brighter the paint is compared to the murals we've been looking at?"

Dee stepped back and pointed to the smaller paintings to the side of the figure. "That's what you saw isn't it?" he said looking at Jamal.

Jamal nodded and turned to look at the painting at the top, to Nicholas's right, it was clearly a scale model of the Winter Palace. Below it was the Great Throne Room. Below that was the Armorial Hall, then the Small Throne Room. At the very bottom, just above the floor was a room painted in gold color with textured walls and a single tile attached at what appeared to be the door of the room.

"Clearly a depiction of Nicholas II, the Winter Palace, and a number of its rooms. There are more rooms down the far side," said Dimitri.

"What does it mean?" asked Mike.

Jamal shook his head.

Dee and Dimitri glanced at one another.

"The gold room is in the Winter Palace, but where?" said Dimitri.

"Could the proximity of the rooms mean something?" asked Jamal.

The others looked to him. He pointed to the top three rooms. "That's where we were. Where I fell. I told you the ceilings didn't look right. That they seemed out of whack. That the halls were different lengths."

"Could that be why those guards were so touchy?" asked Mike.

"Maybe," replied Dimitri. "But I've never heard anything about a gold room and I've been around Russian security for quite some time. Secrets don't usually stay secret for long."

Dee dropped to his knees to examine the painting of the golden room. He stared and turned his head in several directions, but nothing came to him, nor did he see anything different. The others were watching him.

He leaned forward. "It's what you said Dimitri, about seeing something different. In all the murals that we have found, we never touched them. Why is the door a tile while nothing else in this painting appears to be?"

There was silence, no one had an answer.

Dee reached out gingerly and touched the tile. He paused for a moment and then pressed a little more firmly and felt it give. There was a faint click but nothing happened. They stood there in silence for a moment. Dee pushed gently again, and the right side of the tile sprang out. He gripped it in his fingers and pulled softly. It came out of the wall a short distance and Dee could see that it was attached to a rod that was also coming out toward him. He continued to pull slowly, and as the rod came out Dee could see it was attached to a wooden box of which the façade was the remainder of the painting of the golden room. Dee pulled once more, and the box slipped from the wall. The painting of the gold room was on the front, along with three wooden sides and a wooden top with a finger hole.

"What can it be?" asked Jamal.

"Are you sure you want to put your finger in there?" asked Mike.

"It could be booby trapped," said Dimitri.

"Shine the light on it," said Dee.

The finger hole was a cutout and did not pass all the way

through the lid. Dee shook it very softly in his hand. The box wasn't heavy. Dee took the flashlight and shone it around the edges of the lid. It was a tight fit. He could not see into the box or any separation with the sides.

"Step back," said Dee.

"You're going to open it?" asked Dimitri.

"Yeah, we've come this far."

He eased his finger into the slot and tugged gently. He could not feel any resistance and the lid lifted straight out. Dee got the first look inside. He turned toward Dimitri and grinned.

"You'll want to see this." He handed Dimitri the box. Dee had let the lid fall back, but it wasn't completely closed.

Dimitri took the box and slowly, cautiously reopened the top. Gazing inside his eyes grew large.

"What is it?" asked Mike.

Jamal touched him on the arm. "Give him a minute."

Dimitri slowly sat the box down and pulled the top off. Sitting inside, lying on a bundle of straw, was a large pearl egg.

"I can't believe it," he whispered. "After all these years. My grandfather was the last one to touch it."

Dee turned as he heard a sound down the hall. "We'd better move fast."

Dimitri grabbed the egg in one hand, and then quickly placed the other hand beneath it. "It's heavier than I thought."

"How do we get it out of here?" asked Jamal.

Dimitri lifted his tee shirt to reveal a mid-sized black fanny pack. He unzipped it and dropped the egg inside.

Dee grabbed the box, slipped the lid back on, and slid the box back into the wall. He closed the tile door and heard a faint click. "Quick take some pictures Jamal."

Jamal snapped the whole wall and then each room individually as the sounds grew closer.

Dimitri pointed in the opposite direction and whispered, "Let's go."

They left the hallway quickly and then began to run. "Circle around and we'll double back to the stairs," said Dimitri.

Making their way through the basement, they stopped every few moments to listen for sounds, and then resumed moving. As they got near the steps to the upper floor, Dimitri motioned for them to stop and waved them against the wall. "Let me take a peek," he said.

He slipped a little farther down the hall from them and stopped, as if listening. Then slowly he lowered himself down and peeked around the corner from just below waist height. He quickly pulled his head back around. Then he walked softly toward them.

"There are guards at the bottom of the stairs, state security types; they're armed with AKs. We can't go out that way."

"What then?" asked Jamal.

Dimitri pointed back down the hall. "There's an emergency exit out of the bell tower. An alarm will go off but we're pretty close to the Metro. We'll have to make a run for it."

"How did they get on to us?" asked Mike.

"Hard to say, maybe the women Dee and I crossed with, maybe with surveillance. We've been in here for several hours. If they had agents upstairs, they would have figured out that we weren't there. That we had to be someplace more specific."

"What happens if they catch us?" asked Dee.

"Hard to say, but it won't be good. Best thing is not to get caught."

"Agreed, but aren't they looking for us now?"

"Probably, but there's always the chance they aren't sure it's us. If we can get back to the ship, we might have an opportunity."

"Could you tell if it's the state or Sergei's men?"

"Couldn't be sure. Probably Sergei's guys, which means we might get away. If it's state, they'll be everywhere. We won't even make it to the Metro. Come on."

He started scrambling down the corridor, headed for the far corner of the Cathedral and the bell tower.

18

DEE & FRIENDS - MOSCOW METRO

A few minutes later they were in the basement under the Bell Tower where the emergency exit was located.

"The Ploshchad Revolyutsii, Plaza of the Revolution or Revolution Square, Metro entrance is just beyond the GUM store. It's on the blue line. Move quickly toward it but don't run. Stay in the shadows as much as you can. It's late afternoon and there will be people milling around and beginning to head home for the day. Mix in with them but keep moving. We'll leave a few seconds apart and meet up inside the Metro entrance. From there maybe we can see how many are following us."

"Could we cut the alarm?" asked Mike.

Dimitri looked up and grinned at him. "And I'm the one who is supposed to be an Intelligence officer."

Mike looked sheepish. "I just mean, I installed a lot of alarms when I was a builder, and most of them aren't that difficult, especially an emergency alarm."

"No," said Dimitri, "It's an excellent idea. The only tool I have is a knife…and a gun, but you're welcome to them."

Mike reached in his pocket. "I always carry a multi tool, old habit."

Dee looked at him, "Who's the Boy Scout now?"

"I just hope it works."

<hr>

They traveled across the Square individually and without incident. They gathered just inside the entrance to the Metro station.

"I stopped just at the edge of the Square and looked back for surveillance," said Dimitri. "I saw two things. Several men came out the emergency door behind us, the guys at the stairs with the weapons, and then coming around from the front, Novak Novachek and a couple of other men. So it looks like we're being pursued by special interest and not the state. That means we might get away. Let's go." He led them down into the station.

"Where are we going?" asked Mike.

As they scurried down the escalator, Dimitri replied, "We'll try to go north and get back to the ship. The Metro serves about nine million people a day. There's over a dozen different lines, over two hundred seventy-five stations, and over two hundred fifty miles of track. Since they're a small group, we'll try to lose them."

"Won't they have someone at the ship waiting?" asked Jamal.

"Most definitely," replied Dimitri.

"What will we do?"

"One problem at a time."

"We should be able to lose them in the Metro?" asked Dee.

"Maybe, it depends on whether or not they have a mobile CCT feed. There are cameras everywhere."

"That can't be good," said Mike.

"Good for them, not for us. But we'll work around it. Stay in a crowd, avoid the cameras when we can, there are blind spots. To answer the first question, where are we going, to the Teatralnaya Station. It has no external exits. It's a transfer station only. We're coming in at the Plaza of the Revolution, blue line, and taking the escalator to Teatralnaya, on the green line."

"The green line is how we came in from the ship wasn't it?" asked Dee.

"Yes."

"So we're going back north on it," added Dee.

"For now, unless we have to detour. We'll be underground almost exclusively. If we get separated, know that if the train is moving out of town, away from downtown, a woman's voice will announce the stations. If the train is moving towards downtown, it will be a man's voice making the announcements."

"So you always know where you are at?" asked Jamal.

"Hopefully, at least the direction."

They had come off the escalator and were moving across the station towards another one.

Dee, Jamal, and Mike could not keep from turning their heads. The floor was black-and-white marble, the hanging lamps bronze and glass, and every few feet there was a vestibule with a bronze statue.

"This place is fantastic. Must have cost a fortune," said Mike.

"Yeah, you were a builder. The Soviets, Stalin specifically, built these early stations in the mid- 1930s. He called them 'underground palaces.' They were supposed to be a testament to Soviet capability. But they used British engineers initially to train their people, then accused the British of espionage and threw them in prison."

"Were they guilty?" asked Jamal.

"Who knows?"

They were moving along another escalator.

"We're coming into the Teatralnaya Station which is for transfer. We're going to the green line."

"Do you think we got away?" asked Dee.

"Probably from that initial group. It depends on how many men Novak has and if they had the CCT feed. We're headed for the Mayakovskaya Station. They could be waiting for us there."

They were moving rapidly through the Teatralnaya Station now.

"This place is as elaborate as the other," said Mike.

"Probably more so, marble columned walls and all that bas-relief along the ceiling, this is one of the nicest stations in the whole system."

"It's so clean," added Jamal.

"Yeah, you don't litter or deface the Metro stations, serious business if you're caught. Plus, the locals are proud of them. They are a tourist destination in their own right. Here we go."

They boarded the green line and a woman's voice announced that the next station would be Tverskaya then Mayakovskaya.

"The Mayakovskaya Station is where you think they might be?" asked Dee.

"It's an enormous station, a good place to pick us up with fewer problems."

"But there'd be more people?" said Jamal.

"Also more space to work in, smaller areas they could herd us to. Plus, again Russians don't want problems, they'll keep moving and we'll disappear in the crowd. The question is whether it's by ourselves or as captives."

"You say it's a huge station?" asked Mike.

"During World War II, the Russians used it as a field hospital and bomb shelter while the Nazis were pounding away above ground. In fact Stalin lived here for some time, and it was the command post for the Russian Army. It's one of the oldest and earliest stations."

"Are all the stations this elaborate?" asked Jamal.

"Most of the older ones. I mean they are all nice. The outlying ones are a little more contemporary and linear. Not as much art or ornamentation, but still very nice. Going back to our problem, Novak will want to head us off before we reach the brown line that circles the city. If we get there, we could go off in any direction. I feel sure they will come at us."

"Do you think they know we've found the egg?" asked Mike.

"I don't see how. But I do think they think we were on to something, so they made a move."

"You're sure it's Novak, the guy who's chasing the egg?" asked Dee.

"I saw him coming around the church."

"You were a long way off," said Jamal.

Dimitri reached under his shirt and pulled out an adjustable pocket-sized telescope. He held it up. "I got a good look."

"Who's the Boy Scout now?" asked Mike.

"Got to be prepared, number one rule in Intelligence work."

———

THEY PASSED THROUGH THE TVERSKAYA STATION WITHOUT incident.

"Not much farther now. We'll sit tight unless we are forced to move. The brown line is about as far away as we just traveled from the last station. If no one bothers us, we'll stay on the green line and ride it to the end, almost to the canal and the ship. We'll walk from there. Here it comes."

The woman's voice announced, "Mayakovskaya Station."

Looking from inside the train all they could see were throngs of people crowding the platform.

"Keep your eyes down, let me watch," said Dimitri, partially shaded by a break in the windows, his head out of sight from the exterior of the train. They all looked down.

"Move on my command, try to keep each other in sight, but mostly, try to stay alive, don't get yourself killed. If they tell you to stop and flash weapons, stop."

"What should we do?" asked Mike.

"The station is a long corridor running along both sides of the track. There are vaulted archways every few feet separating the corridor from the platform. In the corridor are large overhead circular lights. There aren't many shadows. Run toward one end or the other. Blend into a crowd if you can. There should be lots of people. Make your way to the end of the tunnel and take the short escalator to the next landing. Get off and circle around and come back down. Try to catch the next train heading out of the city. Get off on the brown line transfer station and wait on the platform."

As the train slowed to a stop, Jamal asked, "What do you see?"

"Here they come, at least two of them, probably two more somewhere nearby. Let's get off the train in pairs, Mike, you and Jamal go right, and then Dee and I will go left. Stay in sight of your partner."

The doors opened, and the men moved into the crowd. The outgoing passengers had to push to clear the train door as the oncoming passengers pressed inward.

"Stay close and follow me. The men I saw are on our side," said Dimitri.

Dee nodded and followed along.

They had traveled a couple of column lengths through the corridor of the subway when Dimitri whispered, "They moved behind us. Pull up beside me and act like we're talking. Move quickly, like we're trying to get home at the end of a long day."

Dee closed ranks and, for the first time, got a quick glance of the men behind them, short-haired, plain faced, muscular, in heavy jackets. They didn't look unusual to Dee, just different. They stood out in an otherwise normal looking crowd.

"Is that look a requirement for the job?" whispered Dee as he slid along beside Dimitri.

"They can't help it. They may not start that way but it's how they all end up. Notice how the crowd parts for them? The people know who they are. The crowd's only question is who are they following and how to be prepared to get out of the way. Walk a little faster."

They were coming up on the small escalator, and Dimitri angled toward it. "Stay close." He scrambled up the short expanse of escalator and stepped behind the wall at the landing, just before the long escalator to the surface. He quickly pulled Dee behind him. "Here's what we're going to do."

Dimitri reached across and grabbed a sign that was attached to a metal pole with a base. It stood in front of a garbage can. "I told you they were serious about cleanliness. When they step off the short escalator and start for the long one, I'm going to slam the lead man in the head with this pole. Hopefully, it will knock him out and backward into the second man and they'll both fall down the steps, which will take them back to the landing. When the first man goes down, you head down the other escalator and jump on the train. It should be about ready to pull out."

"What are you going to do?"

"Follow right behind you."

"What about Jamal and Mike?"

"Hopefully these were the only two. I didn't see any others, but I would have expected them. There may not have been enough time to get more of them here, or there may not have been enough of them. They probably expected to capture us at the Square."

Dee leaned forward and saw the men approaching the short escalator. "Here they come."

Dimitri pushed him back against the wall. "Be ready."

As the first man reached the top of the short escalator, he looked back slightly at his partner. Both men had pulled older Makarov pistols and had them clutched upright in their hands. The man took a step onto the landing as Dimitri sprang around the corner and, swinging the metal pole like a baseball bat, connected with the side of the man's head. He went down and into the man behind him causing them both to fall.

"Run," screamed Dimitri.

Dee sprang down the steps of the opposite escalator with Dimitri right behind him. They reached the bottom stair and raced for the train. They crossed through the archway and onto the platform. Starting for the nearest car they saw Mike standing in a doorway further down. They pivoted and started for him as a shot rang out and marble chips from the archway showered down upon them. Dimitri turned just enough to see one of the men while pulling his own pistol from a belly holster.

The man was still running but slowing down. Rather than stop and return fire, Dimitri dove through the opening as the doors began to close.

Dee could see the agent on the platform stop and watch as the train pulled away.

"Why didn't he jump on board?" asked Mike.

"Didn't want to leave his downed partner or start a sustained chase which would draw a lot more attention from regular state security. He wasn't going to take a chance. They know where we are, and they'll be coming again."

"What do we do?" asked Jamal.

"First thing, did you guys see anyone?" asked Dimitri.

"No, we just walked to the escalator, rode up, turned around, rode back, and walked to the train. It's why we were here before you," answered Mike.

"Good, maybe they're stretched thin, and we have a better chance. We're going to jump to the brown line, which should be coming up soon, then ride south. They'll be expecting us to continue north, and we might buy a little time or even give them the slip. We'll jump on the blue line at some point and ride back north toward the canal."

Dee saw blood on the side of Dimitri's neck. "You okay?"

Dimitri rubbed his neck and then went to his fanny pack. "Marble chips, or chunks I should say. Didn't quite get out of the way. Good thing he was running. Those guys are usually pretty good shots." He swabbed the cut with a handkerchief and then held pressure on it. "Hopefully, it's more of a scrape and the bleeding will slow down."

The train was stopping. "Okay, stay close together and along the walls. Look at the floor and follow the man in front of you. I'll lead. We could use a change of clothes or a different look, but there's not much chance of that until we get off the Metro."

Dimitri took point and as the doors opened, he stepped onto the platform and led them to the nearest wall. He followed along beside it and down the platform. As it was ending, he stepped inside to the corridor and remained on the wall moving toward the nearest escalator.

"We'll head south on the brown line, which circles the city. Going counter-clockwise, a woman's voice will announce the stations. Going clockwise it's a man's voice. We can catch the blue line at Kiyevskaya. There are two stops before that, keep a sharp eye."

They sat in silence. Dimitri dabbed at his neck and the others stared off into the distance.

"You think our wives got to the ship?" asked Jamal.

"I imagine. They're pretty timely and wouldn't want to be left behind. Angelic is a control freak. You know she's going to keep them in line," replied Dee.

Jamal grinned.

"Plus Keno is a scaredy cat. She's not going to take a chance," added Mike.

Dimitri looked at them and grinned. "I'm glad you know your wives so well. I expect they know you too. We need them to be on the ship or there could be other problems."

The train eased into the first stop. It sat for several minutes and then got underway again.

"No issues there," said Mike.

"Not that we saw," replied Dimitri.

The train rolled along, moving farther south.

"It'll be a few more minutes until our station. We'll try the same transfer procedure as we did for the brown line. Hopefully, we get onto the blue line and get back to the canal."

19

DEE & FRIENDS - STILL TRAINING

"There are pedestrian crossings on this transfer, where you are outside, in the open air, and walk between stations. We'll get out on the second one just past Kiyevskaya Station and take the cross over back to it. Then board the blue line. If we're lucky, maybe, they'll think we stayed on the brown line and continued to circle around the city."

"We're out in the open, will that be a problem?" asked Jamal.

"The platforms and crossovers are usually really crowded, especially this time of day. It's one of the few things we have working for us."

A female voice came over the PA system and announced the transfer platform to the azure line.

"We're up next for the blue line," said Dimitri as he slipped the bloody handkerchief back into his fanny pack.

The voice came back up again and announced the transfer platform for the blue line.

"This is another really beautiful station, marble floors and walls, colonnade, oil paintings between each of the columns, very ornate, and it has more floor space, more levels and seating around the platforms. Pay attention, there are lots of places for them to hide."

"How will they have found us?" asked Dee.

"If they do, it confirms they have a post or an op center where they're relaying information to the field. It's about the only thing that explains how they've kept up with us."

They were striding across the platform now, heading toward the blue line. They blended into the crowds, staying a few feet apart, but clearly in each other's sight.

Entering the station Dee, Jamal, and Mike couldn't help but glance quickly around at the massive and magnificent interior and the crowds.

"Maybe it is busy enough to lose them," whispered Jamal to Dimitri.

"We can dream."

A few strides later Dimitri stepped into one of the recessed areas between the columns and motioned the others to follow. "They're up in front of us about thirty yards, sweeping through the crowd."

Dee, Jamal, and Mike all stood silently, looking at Dimitri, who had paused and sat on one of the marble benches.

"We'll stay in this alcove. Two to a column on the far side. Maybe they'll pass us by."

"And if they don't?" asked Dee.

"We'll have to deal with it."

They stood silently for a moment and then Dimitri rose. He pointed across the corridor from their alcove. Between two of the arches, there were two raised steps which led to a wall with a painting of a crowd of people. It was as if the viewer could step into the room with them.

"I'm going to go stand on the top step by that painting and hold real still as if I'm part of it and wait for them to pass. You all watch from behind the column, and when they go by, head back the way they came."

"Won't they search the alcove?" asked Mike.

"Probably, but if they start that way I'll cut them off and then you run."

"Do you think standing in front of that painting can really work?" asked Dee.

"Probably not, but it allows me to see them coming, and that's what's important to getting you out of here alive."

Dimitri moved across the corridor and took his place. Mike, Dee, and Jamal gathered behind the nearest pillar with Dee watching the crowd and Dimitri.

Dee noted Dimitri had one hand on his midsection and the other hand frozen close to his body, as if pointing. Dee heard the men before he saw them. There was muttering in Russian and breathing heavily. Dee drew back.

The men roared halfway across Dee's field of vision and for a second he thought their plan might work. Then the man closest noted the alcove and pulled to a stop. His motion caused the other man to actually note Dimitri standing in front of the painting. For a moment, he had looked like part of the painted crowd. That man broke for Dimitri as the other stepped into the alcove.

As they heard his steps coming toward them, Dee, Jamal, and Mike eased around the column, keeping away from him. He walked just far enough to look on the backside and then turned toward the corridor again.

They heard a sound, like a small firework or a hammer banging on metal, and Dee looked out from behind the column. He saw Dimitri with a suppressed pistol in his hand holding up the other man and swinging him around so that he leaned against the wall. The man who had been checking the alcove reached for his pistol and called out in Russian. Dimitri raised his pistol and fired again. The man stumbled backward into the column where the others hid.

Dee glanced over to Dimitri who quickly holstered the pistol and pointed with his head toward the train.

"Let's go," Dee whispered to the others. As they came around the column and saw the man lying on the floor, Dee held up a hand. "Grab his feet and arms. Pull him behind the column and then head for the train." The three of them quickly pulled the man out of sight and then crossed the corridor to the platform and joined Dimitri in the car.

"We pulled him out of sight," said Mike.

"Thanks," said Dimitri. They all sat silently for a moment as the train pulled away.

Dee could see that Dimitri was breathing deeply, as if trying to calm himself. Dee was still trying to absorb what had happened and hadn't panicked yet. Jamal and Mike sat silently, as if the weight of the situation was bearing on them.

"We've got to get to the boat," said Dimitri. "It's serious now. We might have talked our way out of it before, but not after that. Novak will want vengeance for his men."

———

They rode in silence, caught their breath, and thought about the situation.

"This part of the blue line runs due east until it gets to Park Pobedy Station. It's one of the newer ones. The design is more contemporary but still lots of marble, glass, colonnade, and oil paintings. It's a shiny stop, new highly polished marble, slick floors. Be careful, running could be a struggle. It's similar to the other stations. Columns along a corridor with the platform on either side. It's the deepest station in the system at two hundred and seventy-five feet. There's really nowhere to run. If they've made their way down to it, we're probably trapped."

"Can't we just stay on the train? You said we turn north from there?" asked Jamal.

"If we're lucky."

"If we see them, should we stay on the train or get off? Mighten we be safer on the train, since it's still nearly full?" said Dee.

"Ideally, yes. It'll be a question of if they force us off."

The train eased into the station, and they could see what Dimitri had been describing. A marble checkerboard floor and curved marble columns that disappeared in the distance in an optical illusion.

But then Dimitri saw them coming and they were quite real. Novak and six of his people, three to either side. The crowd parted like the sea before Moses.

"Stay still, don't run. There's almost too many people to make a scene. Let's see what he has to say. At least then we'll know."

"You getting tired?" asked Dee as he noticed the blood running down the side of Dimitri's face again. Jamal and Mike looked anxiously out the window.

"Yeah, I am." He handed Dee his fanny pack. "Keep this. Hide it quick."

Dee slipped it on and pulled his shirt over it without Jamal or Mike observing him.

Novak stopped at the door closest to being in front of Dimitri and the others. Three men had peeled off at the door before and three men went to the door beyond. They entered the train and approached Dimitri's group from both sides.

The largest and closest man spoke, "Get off the train… now!"

Dimitri nodded and all four of the men rose and stepped out the center door in front of Novak.

"Dimitri," said Novak. "Fancy running into you in the deepest hole under Moscow. What manner of foolishness have you been up to?" He waved a hand at Dee, Jamal, and Mike. "And you brought friends."

"What do you want Novak?"

"Why the same as you, the egg. It's what we all want."

"Why are you chasing me? I know less than you."

"I've never quite believed that—you, your father, your grandfather—you're too close to it. What were you doing in the church?"

Dimitri glanced at the others. "I was helping my friends. We met on the river cruise, and they had an interest in historical Russian religious art."

"Why don't I believe that."

"It's true," said Jamal. "I'm an art historian."

"Right now you are just going to be silent. You are not part of this conversation."

Jamal took a step back as Novak's men had taken a step forward.

"Really Dimitri? This is all so trivial. The fact that you even look for the egg. We knew you were there when we killed your father. You were so inconsequential we didn't even bother with you. Your little double agent charade, do you not realize that we have been on to you for years, as have the Americans. Each side feeds you some meaningless detail that you report back and forth and we all have a good laugh. You were too inconsequential to even terminate. You've stumbled around in the dark for years. Yes, I killed your grandfather too. He was equally foolish. The only question I have now is, should I bother to kill you today? Are you even worth a bullet? Ordinarily I'd have said no, but you killed three of my men."

"Three?"

"The one you hit with the sign, snapped his neck, and the two you shot. My men demand justice. Plus, I'm tired of having you around. I'll simply report that you reacted violently to some simple questions and had to be put down, like a rabid dog, a toothless rabid dog."

Dimitri took a step toward Novak with his hands outstretched to the side. Novak's men closed in around him. Dee, Jamal, and Mike took a step backward and closer to the train.

"I'm tired too," said Dimitri. "I've had enough." He lunged forward as if to strike Novak and the men surrounding Novak closed in further to grab Dimitri.

"Jump on the train," yelled Dimitri.

Dee, Jamal, and Mike pivoted, took a single step, and jumped into the train car, landing on the floor as the doors closed. Several of the men fired shots through the glass. It sprinkled around the men on the floor as the train pulled away.

Several of Novak's men jumped for the train but he raised a hand. "No, gather Dimitri up and let's get out of here before there is any more chaos or confusion on the Metro tonight. We don't want other state security snooping around."

20

DEE & FRIENDS - BOUND FOR
THE BOAT

"What do you think they'll do to him?" asked Mike.

"Sounded a lot like they were going to kill him," replied Jamal.

They rode in silence for several moments.

"I think we take this to the end of the line. There's six or eight stations and then it terminates. We should be close to the canal. We'll have to find our way," said Dee.

"Do you think there will be men waiting?" asked Jamal.

"I hope not. Maybe Novak got what he wanted in Dimitri. We'll have to pay attention."

"Think they'll just kill him and dump the body?" asked Mike.

"Maybe, if he's lucky. They might torture him, which could be long and painful, and possibly hazardous to us. We don't really know anything. But still. They may not want any loose ends."

"We're supposed to fly out late tomorrow I heard Angelic say," said Jamal.

"Can't be soon enough," added Mike. "But I wish there was some way we could help Dimitri."

———

NOVAK'S MEN FROG-MARCHED DIMITRI TOWARD THE escalator.

"Why do you persist with this Dimitri?" asked Novak.

"It's my family legacy."

"Not much of one. If your family had the egg, they would have brought it forward by now. I will find it."

"Why do you care so much? I mean Sergei, I understand. He was once accused of stealing it, and that cloud never quite dissipated."

"Nonsense, he had nothing to do with it. Anastasia or one of the other royal family members disposed of it in some fashion."

"What about the dagger? He certainly took that. I saw it with my own eyes right before you killed my father."

"Too bad about that. It was a nice knife, the czar's, good enough for the Imperial crest. Shame it fell in the lake."

"Yeah, too bad about that."

Novak kicked Dimitri in the back of the thigh from behind. "You will tell us what you know before the night is through."

Dimitri stumbled and then turned to look at him. "Not a chance." Novak punched his cheek right below the eye before Dimitri could turn away. "I don't know anything."

They reached the escalator in a few steps and began the long ascent to the surface. The escalator was steep as it had to climb two hundred and fifty feet. Novak's men pushed Dimitri in front of them and lined up behind him with Novak last.

About thirty feet up, Dimitri stepped up beside the man in front of him. A businessman from the looks of him. The escalator was very crowded as it was late in the day and people were hurrying home.

Novak's men behind Dimitri were chatting and laughing about something. Dimitri leaned closer to the man beside him and whispered, "I'm sorry." Then he shoved the man hard backwards. The stumbling man hit the first two of Novak's men and set off a domino effect that Dimitri didn't wait around to see. He hopped up over the handrail and onto the surface between the two escalators and ran upward as fast as he could. About fifty feet beyond, Dimitri took a quick look back and people were still sprawled about and picking themselves up. He increased his speed and raced for the top.

———

They reached the end of the blue line at Pyatnitskoe Shosse. It was the terminating point and a very simple station, marble floors, square columns, no art. It could have been anywhere in the world. Exiting quickly they went up the escalator and onto the street. Huddling in an outer plaza, they had to make a decision.

"Let's go back inside and look for a Metro map," said Dee.

"Do we want to risk being seen?" asked Jamal.

"I'll go. You two stay here and keep an eye out for any more of Novak's thugs."

Dee disappeared inside the station. Jamal and Mike stayed close to the building in the shadow of some shrubbery.

Only a few minutes later Dee reemerged and approached them. "The canal is an hour due north of here, so much for being close. I suggest we take a taxi." He pointed. "There seem to be plenty of them. We'll stop a few blocks short. It's a main highway. There should be some place we can get out."

"Find one that speaks English," suggested Mike.

They headed toward the cab stand and looked at the cars.

There were two that had English signs on the door. Dee approached the first one.

"Can you take us out toward the Moscow Canal?" asked Dee.

"It's about an hour but no problem as long as you can pay."

Dee took out a couple of $20s. "This get us started? Can you let us out about a half mile before you get there?"

"It's not a very safe area that far out. Nearer to the docks is safer."

Dee, Jamal, and Mike glanced at each other. Dee, riding shotgun, looked back at the driver.

Before he could speak, the driver offered, "I can take you over a couple of streets and let you out right at the end of the docks. Won't take you but a minute to find your ship and you'll feel like you're walking."

"It's a tourist thing?" asked Dee.

"Yeah, people think they're safe. Not even in daylight. You be careful."

———

THEY WALKED THE DOCK SLOWLY, STAYING OUT OF THE LIGHT and watching for people. They saw very little. Occasionally a voice made its way out of the darkness but never directed at them. When they reached the ship, they took a quick glance around and could see nothing that posed an issue. They scrambled quickly aboard and went to the Panorama Bar. Dee texted Gina and asked her to get the other women and come to meet them.

The men were sitting in the bar, their backs to the bulkhead where they could see in either direction. The night's events had made an impression. They looked tired and gaunt.

"You guys all right?" asked Angelic as she approached and sat opposite Jamal.

"We've been better, but we're glad to be here. Did you have any trouble getting back to the ship?"

"Not a bit," said Gina. "We did spend quite a bit of money," she followed with a smile. "We had too much time on our hands when you guys didn't come back."

"Yeah, big guy," said Keno as she rubbed Mike's shoulder. "What's up?"

"We had a really unusual adventure and some security guys that Dimitri knew carried him away. He helped us to escape."

"What?" said all three women at the same time.

"Tell us more," said Angelic.

"It's a long story," answered Jamal.

"Just give them the highlights," said Dee.

"Okay," replied Jamal. "We found the painting, we found the egg, we were chased by bad guys, we ran all over the Metro —subway, Dimitri got captured and we got away. Here we are. Don't know what to do next."

21

DEE & FRIENDS - NESTING

They sat and chatted for a while and filled their wives in on all the details.

"Let's go down to our stateroom. I want to show you guys something," said Dee.

They followed him down and sat in a circle in the living room.

"What's the big deal?" asked Mike.

Jamal was sitting beside Dee, rubbing his hands together. "I know it's going to be good."

Dee raised his shirt, and the women drew back slightly. "Yeah, I need a shower, but that's not what I want to show you." He unzipped the fanny pack and pulled out the Fabergé egg.

"When did he give it to you?" asked Jamal.

"Is that really it?" asked Gina.

"When we were on the train. You guys were looking out the window. Novak and his men were approaching."

"He must have known," said Mike.

"He passed it off just before they took him, didn't he?" said Angelic.

Dee nodded and handed the egg to Jamal. "You're the closest thing we have to an art expert. What do you think?"

"Short answer, it's a masterpiece, one of only two in the world, made exclusively for the czar. Unbelievable that we have it in our possession."

"Or that Dimitri gave his life for it," added Mike.

"There was nothing you could do?" asked Keno.

"Probably would have gotten us all killed," replied Mike.

Jamal had been examining the egg while the others talked. He raised a hand.

"Look, I think there's a seam." He held the egg up for the others to see. "Right here, just below the center." He twisted and jiggled the egg. "Last thing I want to do is damage or break a priceless artifact."

He kept finagling the egg back and forth, up and down. Slowly a space appeared and then quickly the egg popped in two. He held the lower portion in one hand and the upper portion in the other. But, inside the lower portion, was another egg. They all looked at it in amazement.

Mike was first to speak. "What is that?"

"It appears to be another egg," replied Jamal. "And I had no idea, there was no sound, it must fit perfectly inside the outer one." He sat both of the exterior pieces on the coffee table and took the inner egg in his hand.

"Why would they do that?" asked Gina.

Dee and Jamal looked at one another. "Russian nesting dolls," they both whispered.

"What?" asked Keno.

"The Russians make dolls, in a round shape, which fit one inside another. Sometimes several of them. What looks like one, you take apart and you have a whole family. Very popular with children," said Jamal.

"Probably with moms too," added Angelic. "Less to keep up with and takes less space."

Jamal was examining the second egg. "I think we're on to something. I think this one is seamed as well."

He kept fiddling with the second egg, the same as he had with the first.

"How did you know to look?" asked Angelic.

Jamal kept fiddling with the egg but replied, "When I was working with Diego in Spain, he said that older artifacts were often multi-parted or integrated in parts. It was a way that older civilizations hid things or attempted to keep them secret. He also said it could be that they were just superb craftsmen."

Jamal continued. "You look at every detail, every item of the piece, and try not to get overwhelmed by the complete artifact or what it represents. Break it down into small pieces and look for differences."

At just that moment, he was able to separate the second egg and once again there was another smaller egg inside.

"How far does this go?" asked Keno.

Jamal shook his head. "I don't know. Some of the nested dolls can be four to six deep."

"Again, why would they do that?" asked Dee. "What was the czar or czarina's purpose in having these made? Why so many?"

"Were they just playing?" asked Gina, "Some kind of private joke?"

"Maybe," replied Jamal. "But let's keep looking." He had taken the third egg and was examining it.

He turned it slowly, looking along the bottom third. Having disassembled two outer layers, he was getting faster at identifying the seam.

"There it is." Jamal began pulling on the third smaller egg. It only took a moment, and he had it apart. Inside was the fourth egg. This one about the size of a chicken egg.

"I don't think they can get much smaller," said Keno.

Jamal began to fiddle with the egg. This one didn't want to

separate. "I don't see or feel a seam. Perhaps this is the final one."

"Why would you put four eggs inside one another?" asked Angelic.

"Tradition?" said Mike. "I mean, if the dolls are that way, and it probably makes the whole thing more valuable. From what we've seen the czars didn't skip much on expense."

Jamal was still working with the egg while the others talked. He couldn't find anything. Then he held it to his ear and shook it.

"Quiet," he said. Everyone stopped talking. He shook the egg again.

"I can hear just the faintest ruffle inside."

"Could it be the way it's made?" asked Angelic.

"Possibly, but I don't think so. I think this was more obvious. It was a way to hide something. I just need to look again."

He held the egg to the light. He twisted it and turned it. He scanned the surface with his fingers, smooth all over.

"Nothing?" asked Dee.

Then Jamal noticed that the top of the egg had a piece of inlaid pearl that was star-shaped, but the bottom of the egg did not. He pressed the star, and the egg hinged open. Inside the bottom was a small piece of scroll.

"What is that?" asked Keno.

Jamal shook his head and sat the egg down very softly. He wiped his fingers on his pants and then touched the edge of the scroll lightly. It felt soft. He picked the scroll up with his fingers and unrolled it. He held it in both hands and looked away from the light. A smile came to his face, and he shook his head slightly.

"What does it say?" asked Dee.

Jamal leaned back and laughed. "Not what you'd think. It

says, 'in the other egg' in some gold-colored script." He held it out for each of them to see.

"What does that mean?" asked Gina.

"What other egg?" asked Keno.

"Do you suppose Anastasia grabbed the wrong egg?" said Mike to Jamal.

"It's possible."

"What do you mean gold script?" asked Dee.

"It's written in a gold liquid, like honey. It has a texture. I have no idea what it is."

They sat talking, asking questions with no answers when Dee's phone vibrated. He pulled it out and looked at the screen, then held up a hand. Everyone fell silent.

"I'll be right there." He rose and continued. "Dimitri is in the bar. He's hurt. I'll go get him. Mike you want to help? Jamal you stay here with the egg, or eggs. Ladies, keep an eye out."

22

DEE & FRIENDS - BACK ON THE BOAT

They returned in a few minutes assisting Dimitri into the room. He had a bad limp, the side of his head was bleeding again, and his right eye was badly swollen and discolored.

"What happened to you?" asked Keno.

Dimitri grinned, revealing a bit of a split lip as well. "I got lucky and got away from Novak. But they'll probably be coming here to look for me or question you."

"What do we do?" asked Mike.

Jamal held up a hand. "I'm glad you made it."

"For now."

"Let me show you this quickly and get your opinion." Jamal pulled the eggs out and then the scroll. "It says, 'in the other egg,' in some gold script that we don't recognize. Mean anything to you?"

Dimitri looked at it for a moment, a blank expression on his face. "I have no idea. Not what I was expecting."

"What were you expecting?" asked Gina.

"I don't really know, but not a riddle or another clue. I thought there would be an answer."

"Could Anastasia have grabbed the wrong egg?" asked Dee.

"It's possible, since we don't know the actual circumstances under which she took it or had it given to her. The other egg, if that's what she means, is in the state museum. They've had it all along."

"Yeah, but do you think they know it's a nesting egg? Would Fabergé have told them?" said Jamal.

"Not likely. Fabergé hated the Bolsheviks. They wouldn't have done anything to enhance or enrich them. The other egg, the mate, has probably sat under glass since the Revolution."

"I'm surprised someone didn't take it," said Gina.

"There was too much awareness and too many competing factions early on. Once it was secured in the Hermitage, it was a lot more visible and difficult to take. I understand there was a lot of pressure on Sergei early on. He was alone in the throne room when it was noticed that one egg was missing."

"What does it mean to you?" asked Dee.

"The egg? The note? I don't know. I wasn't sure I'd ever find it. I'm grateful to you all. It's a bit of a letdown. Just another riddle. I'm not sure we can get to the other egg, but now we have to try to get back to St. Petersburg, for the gold room and the egg."

"We're supposed to fly out tomorrow morning," said Angelic.

"Where to?"

"Maldives."

"Ah, should be nice—warm, sunny beaches, nothing to do but lie in the sand and enjoy the sun and surf."

"Not just yet," said Dee. "We need to see this through."

"Are you crazy?" asked Mike. "He was nearly killed."

"Yeah, he was, but he wasn't. He can't do this without help. I think you, Keno, Gina, and Angelic should fly on to the islands. Jamal and I will stay here and help Dimitri."

"Not a good idea," said Dimitri. "There aren't many ways this can end well."

"Are you just going to quit and run?" asked Jamal.

"No, despite what Novak said about me, this is my life. I owe it to my family and myself to see it through."

"How would you go about that?" asked Dee.

"The only card I have left to play. I know the Hermitage Museum director personally. We're old friends, his family was in the priesthood as well. We met years ago and have much in common. His allegiance is to the art, not to the state. I think he will help me. How public it becomes is up to him. But at least we will have an answer."

"So, we have to get back to St. Petersburg. How?" asked Dee.

"You can't be serious about doing this," said Angelic.

"I don't like it," said Gina.

Dimitri held up his hands. "I understand and I agree. I think it foolish for your husbands to stay."

"See," said Angelic.

Jamal turned to Dimitri and asked, "How are you going to do it?"

"I need to get back to St. Petersburg. Everything, transportation wise, will be monitored. I found a couple of small boats that can get us, me, back up the canal to the Volga. From there I can make my way back surreptitiously."

"You said 'us'," said Dee.

"I misspoke."

"You also said boats, plural," said Jamal.

Dimitri touched the side of his face where the dried blood had caked. "I didn't know what you all would want to do. But I knew that one small boat wouldn't hold us all and that you didn't need to travel with me. Too dangerous. Novak let you escape earlier tonight. Were there any of his men here at the ship?"

"Not that we saw," said Mike.

"That's good. He may actually have believed a little of your story about the church paintings. I know he's obsessed with me. So we shouldn't travel together. Leaving is probably best."

Jamal looked at Dee. "We want—need—to know the answer."

"You must be prepared for the consequences."

"If we travel separately, we can deny everything."

"That's only a small chance at best. I need to go, before Novak recovers."

"If you carry the egg and he catches you, he'll kill you."

"He'll probably kill me anyway. Sergei's infatuation with my family is probably the only thing that kept me alive all these years."

"We have to carry the egg," said Dee. Jamal nodded his agreement. "Mike, take everyone and fly to the Maldives. We'll be there as soon as we can. Dimitri has a plan that seems workable."

"You guys are not serious," said Keno.

"We are," said Dee.

"And we will be careful," added Jamal.

23

DEE & FRIENDS - UP THE RIVER

After saying goodbye to the others and thanking them for their help, Dimitri led Dee and Jamal to the Panorama Bar. They sat in the back by the wall.

"I have a couple of small boats two docks up toward the end of the landing," said Dimitri.

"We walked in that way from the road," replied Jamal. "We can find them."

"Okay, I need to go on in case Novak and his men come looking. I'll go now. You guys leave in the morning. It'll be easier for you."

Dee and Jamal both looked at him.

"It won't be dark, and I know where I'm going. You'll need landmarks, plus it separates us so if Novak comes by here, you look like you're on your way out of town. It might encourage him to let you go."

"Where are we headed?" asked Jamal.

"Upriver, beyond the next small town. There are some landmarks to let you know you're getting close. The actual meeting place is less prominent."

"What are we looking for?" asked Dee.

"On your starboard there will be a small seawall. It will have a built-in dock and stairs. Going away from it are a walkway and more stairs to a landing where an old mansion used to be. Now it's overgrown with brush and trees. Just beyond it you can pull into a cove and anchor your boat and make your way to the ruins. With me so far?"

They both nodded.

"Now to get there, this is what you are going to do. Man your craft and head north out of the city. Pretty quickly you'll cross under the Dimitry Highway Bridge and on your starboard will be the Admiral Yacht Club. Continue north and a few miles later you'll come to the Troitsk Yacht Club, Recreation Center, and Troitsk Pier, all on the starboard. Start paying close attention at that point. Your last landmark will be the Church of the Holy Trinity and just beyond that will be the seawall, all on the starboard. It shouldn't take you more than an hour or two. If it's longer than that, you're lost." He grinned.

"What do we need to bring?" asked Jamal.

"Clothing for a couple of days, passports, personal items, but try to keep it light. We'll have to move fast."

"How long will it take us to get to St. Petersburg?" asked Dee.

"It's five days by water but we should be able to make it in no more than three. I have a couple of ideas that might cut it shorter."

"How?" asked Jamal.

"What's that they say, the less you know the better, especially if Novak shows up tonight or in the morning. I'd leave early. Pack up tonight and say goodbye. Slip out in the morning and leave them sleeping. If they're accosted by Novak, the less they know the better."

He paused, but then continued, "Are you sure you want to do this? It's about to get very real. It could go smoothly, but it could blow up in our faces, which probably means your death. Those are some smart, good-looking women to leave widowed, and what looks like a comfortable lifestyle you lead."

"All that's true, but we need to see this through," said Jamal.

"We've come too far," added Dee.

"Well, I can't thank you enough. I've been searching for this all my life, this moment and what it means, I can't even really explain it to you."

"That's okay, you don't have to."

———

DEE AND JAMAL WENT BACK TO THEIR ROOMS AND PACKED quickly, each of them placing everything in a small shoulder bag.

"Baby, I wish you wouldn't go," said Gina. "But I can see you're going to. Be careful, come back to me. I'll be wearing that blue thong on the beach in the Maldives."

"You know I'll be back. I wouldn't miss you or that for the world."

Over in Jamal's cabin, it was a little more heated.

"Are you out of your mind?" said Angelic. "You don't have to do this."

"Yes, I do. This is my life now. Ever since I worked with Diego on all those artifacts, I have to know. I'll be careful and I'll be back."

"You better be. I'm not done with you."

———

THEY SLIPPED OUT AT DAWN THE NEXT MORNING WITHOUT waking either of their wives. Walking down the dock toward their boat, Jamal said, "You going to leave them a message?"

"Yeah, but nothing too specific." Dee texted Mike a cryptic, 'see you at the beach, travel safe.'

"We probably are crazy," said Jamal.

"Definitely," replied Dee. "But we're still doing it."

"Yeah, we are."

They reached the small motorboat only to note that it had a 225-horsepower inboard motor.

"Nice boat, wonder where he got it?" asked Jamal.

"I don't know but it might have something to do with him telling us to leave early. Let's get underway. I'll drive, you navigate."

"Dimitry Highway Bridge coming up first."

They started slow, as Dee got a feel for the controls, then picked up some speed.

"We don't want to attract any attention," called out Dee.

"Yeah, two non-Russians zooming up the canal at dawn-thirty. Nothing unusual about that."

They had risen and eaten an early breakfast for the last time on the longship. No one had mentioned that Dee and Jamal were no longer with them.

"We need to get a move on," said Mike. "The flight is almost ten hours. It'll be early evening before we get there."

Gina turned toward him. "Do you suppose…"

"What?" asked Mike.

"There's someone coming," she replied.

"Everyone stay calm," whispered Mike.

Two burly men approached. They stopped beside the table and the closest one spoke. "So, you are leaving today?"

Mike replied, "Yes, very shortly. We need to get to the airport. We have a long flight."

"That is a good thing," said the second man.

"We enjoyed our stay," replied Mike. "But it's time to go."

The first man glanced around the table. "Where are the other two?"

No one spoke for a second. Then Gina popped up. "As you can see, we're about finished. They were going to the restroom and then back to the stateroom to get the luggage. We don't want to be late."

"No, you don't," said the second man, "want to miss your flight."

The men turned and left.

Everyone sat very still for a few moments. "You heard the man," said Mike. "Let's get our stuff and get out of here."

———

THEY HAD PASSED THE ADMIRAL YACHT CLUB AND WERE JUST motoring beyond the Troitsk trio of the yacht club, recreation center, and pier.

"We have a church and then we start looking?" asked Dee. "Is that right?"

Jamal nodded while not taking his eyes away from the shore. It was a bright sunny day, not a cloud in a clear blue sky. They had passed a couple of other boats and a barge heading into the city and had been passed by a big twin engine outboard moving along at top speed.

"I never thought of Russia and boating," said Jamal. "I mean two yacht clubs, lots of river traffic. They must love the water."

"Only in the summer," replied Dee.

They had been traveling about an hour and a half when a church tower came into sight.

"I think that's it," called Jamal. "Slow it down and let's start looking."

They continued moving along comfortably, just two men

out on a boat ride. Jamal pointed and Dee nodded. The seawall wasn't difficult to spot. They eased past it at the same speed and then cut into a small cove just beyond. Dee edged the boat toward the bank and Jamal jumped out onto a small wooden landing.

"Not really a dock, more like an observation point," said Jamal.

"Yeah, but we're out of sight," replied Dee.

Jamal tied them off, and they disembarked.

"What now?" asked Jamal.

"Head for the ruins, stay in the weeds," replied Dee.

They had only traveled a few feet when Dimitri appeared from behind a tree with a pistol in his hand. "Good to see it's only you," he said. He holstered the pistol. "Any problems?"

"Smooth trip, didn't see or hear anything," answered Jamal. "Did you have any trouble?"

"Got a little tired about halfway but no incidents."

"Looks like we need to get you cleaned up a bit," said Dee.

"That would be helpful. When I got here, I just crawled among the ruins and passed out. I've been up since daylight, waiting for you."

"What now?" asked Jamal.

"There's a little settlement near the church you passed. We'll head back there to get a few things. We need to get to the other end of the canal. I think you have the nicer, faster boat. We'll take it."

"Where'd you get the boats?" asked Dee.

Dimitri leaned against a tree and grinned. "I borrowed them."

"We suspected as much," said Jamal.

"No one should be looking for them this far up the canal. We'll ditch the one here and the other when we get back to the Volga. It's not far."

24

DEE & FRIENDS - WHERE THE WATER MEETS THE SKY

A short time later, they had been to the general store in the settlement and purchased some towels and washcloths, bandages, a couple of shirts, and three pairs of hiking boots. The young woman who waited on them had been pleasant and wished them well.

"I'm glad we didn't try to do that without you," said Dee to Dimitri. "She was talky, and my Russian is non-existent."

"They don't get too many tourists this far from the city. Jamal stayed on the boat, you nodded at her and let me talk. That was enough. My Russian is good enough, I am Russian, and she had no reason to be suspicious. My bruises were enough for her to avoid asking too many questions. Just be nice and smile and forget about it."

They were back on the boat and headed north toward the Volga conflux.

"A few miles short of the Volga, we'll ditch the boat and go on foot for a little ways. I know a safe place."

"Do you think Novak will be looking for you or us?" asked Jamal.

"He might send a couple of men to the longship to be sure your group is leaving."

"What if they find us missing?" asked Dee.

"We have to hope your friends were clever, or he'll be after all three of us. I don't really think he had a deep suspicion of you."

"Why not? I mean back at Yaroslavl Park it got pretty tense."

"Agreed, but his men at the museum were suspicious of you, which is why they followed you. I don't think he connected your fall or mural search or research with the egg. You were just unlucky when you fell that it happened to be in front of one of his men. Russian security men have a natural paranoia about them. I have it too. Besides, you're supposed to be leaving the country. I think he was more worried about me finding the egg."

"I still don't understand why it matters to him."

"I think it's just the hunt. The resolution to a hundred plus year old mystery. It will boost his status in the security service and make him known around the country. The political and security guys strive to be recognized by the people."

"Not admired?"

"No, just recognized."

———

THEY APPROACHED THE END OF THE MOSCOW CANAL, AND Dimitri directed them into a small landing.

"We'll abandon the boat here," said Dimitri. "Maybe we can catch a ride. The place I'm looking for is not far."

They didn't catch a ride, so they walked for a time. It was rural, and no one passed them along the road.

"Probably less than a kilometer now," said Dimitri.

"A kilometer." Jamal laughed. "How is it speaking two languages fluently? Do you find you mix words occasionally?"

"We would have called the distance in miles," added Dee.

Dimitri grinned at them and then sighed and wiped his forehead. "I didn't used to. You had to be very careful to use the correct idioms. In the last few years, I've noticed myself slipping. It's time to retire."

"What will you do?" asked Dee.

"I don't really know. I have no family. Maybe I'll go teach sailing on the Great Lakes."

Dee and Jamal both looked at him, surprise on their faces.

"I'm just teasing you guys. I haven't sailed since I was a kid."

"Since your dad?" asked Jamal.

Dimitri nodded. "I'll find something, although without my work, actually my quest for the egg, it won't have much meaning." He trudged on for a moment and then pointed at a windsock across the nearby field.

"There, that's where we want to be."

They trudged across the field, Dimitri leading the way. "Just look nonchalant. Like this is an everyday thing for you."

Stepping inside the hanger, Dimitri paused for a moment and then threw up an arm to a man on the far side. "Wait here." He walked across the open space and greeted the man.

"So, you think we're going to fly to St. Petersburg?" said Jamal.

"Looks that way, possibly. It would certainly be faster than walking."

A few minutes later, the men walked across the hangar to join them. Dimitri spoke to the man in Russian and pointed, "Dee," and pointed again, "Jamal."

The man nodded, wiped his hands on his pants and shook hands, then walked away.

At the far end of the hangar sat an old twin engine Beechcraft. The man was walking toward it.

Dimitri turned to them. "He flies cargo at low altitude between here and St. Petersburg, occasionally to Moscow."

"Something significant about low altitude?" asked Dee.

"Stay out of restricted airspace and less of a presence to be observed. He just has to pay attention to other low-flying craft."

"He's taking us?" asked Jamal.

"We're riding along. It's a cargo plane, no seats, no seat belts, no parachutes, no stewardesses, budget class."

"Did it cost?" asked Dee.

"I gave him a couple of hundreds I had in my sock."

"You know this guy?" asked Jamal.

"Yeah, he's an acquaintance, maybe friend, I met him on the St. Petersburg end when I was spending a lot of time around my grandfather's old church. He doesn't fly directly into St. Petersburg, which is good, but lands in a similarly rural location and trucks the freight."

"So we're safe?" asked Jamal.

"We should be, unless there's an air accident. He's a good pilot. I've ridden with him before."

"How soon do we leave?" asked Dee.

"As soon as we get over there and find a place to sit. He was about to leave. I was hoping we'd catch him on this end. He usually flies down and back each day."

"How long?" asked Dee.

"A little over two hours in his plane, depending on the volume of freight."

"We're getting back fast," said Jamal.

"Yeah, we want to get this done as quickly as we can and get you guys out of the country."

"What about you?" asked Dee.

"Maybe I'll come with you."

25

DEE & FRIENDS - SKYWARD

Three hours later they found themselves on the ground at a little rural airstrip outside St. Petersburg. It hadn't been a bad flight. They'd sat on the freight compartment floor and leaned against some of the boxes. It had been a full load. They had looked forward and seen out the cockpit window as the pilot made his way toward St. Petersburg. He had flown it solo.

They hadn't been able to talk during the flight as the noise had been so loud. On the ground with their ears still slightly ringing Jamal asked, "Does he always fly solo? Aren't there rules?"

"There are and he does have a co-pilot, but they often make the run alone. It's not that far and there's good weather. Sometimes one of them has something to do. You saw that we never got above one thousand feet. We weren't much more than tree-top fliers."

"Yeah, but we're here, what now?" asked Dee.

"We need to get into the city and contact my friend at the museum."

"Would it be better to contact him beforehand? Let him know we're coming?" asked Jamal.

"Probably not, the less he knows the better. Let me see if I can arrange with one of the freighters. Get us a ride into town."

"Need money?" asked Dee.

"Would improve our chances. American currency is still highly valued in this country."

Dee handed him a roll of bills.

"I'll be back."

A few seconds later Dimitri walked about halfway to them and waved a hand. "Come on, we got a ride."

Less than an hour later they pulled into the freight terminal and exited the truck. They waved to the driver and slipped into the crowd outside the perimeter fence.

"Any reason we rode all the way in?" asked Dee.

"It was as good a place as any. Not a lot of state security out this far, lots of payoffs but not much presence. We'll have to be cautious from here on."

"How do we go about contacting your friend?" asked Jamal.

"Cautiously. I'm confident that he will help, but we can't put him in any kind of compromise or danger."

"Do you think Novak is looking for you, or us?" asked Dee.

"I would imagine. He's never given up. I thought after Sergei died Novak might walk away, but he hasn't. In fact, he's been more vigilant than ever. So yes, I expect he's out there."

"Where can we stay, or hide, while you're trying to reach your friend?" asked Jamal.

"I know several safe houses, but they'd all be compromised. When I worked out of this area I had a place, but I let it go when I moved to Moscow. Sergei or someone ransacked it several times."

"So they did know about you?" said Dee.

"Yes, there was a general awareness. It may have been more to do with the double agent thing early on. I've been suspicious for some time now. I stopped getting relevant information, from either side, several years ago."

He continued. "There is this place I rented that I never used. I've never even been there. I kept it when I left the area. I'm over here a couple of times a year, so whenever I am in the area, I pay them in cash. Gave them a fake name."

"Your own safe house," said Dee.

"Something like that. You have to have a plan in this country if you want to stay alive."

"If you've never been there, how do we get inside?" asked Jamal.

"I have a P.O. box nearby where I keep a key."

"You're a real 'Red October' aren't you?"

Dimitri grinned then said, "You watch too many cheesy movies."

"How will you reach your friend?" asked Dee.

"Well, my safe house is across town from the museum, which is unfortunate. But the museum would be too risky anyway as a direct approach. I know where he lives, and I'll go over at night and catch up with him."

"Does he have family? A wife, children?" asked Jamal.

"He has a wife but she won't be there."

"How do you know that?" asked Dee.

"She's a teacher. She tutors a number of the Politburos' offspring in Moscow."

"Does he see her very often?" asked Jamal.

"No, in fact he sees her rarely. She also entertains members of the Politburo."

"He knows this?" asked Dee.

"Oh, yes."

"And he's okay with it?" asked Jamal.

"He doesn't have a lot of choice and the relationships

provide him a certain immunity in his job. If he complained, he would surely lose it."

"All the more reason he might help us," said Dee.

Dimitri nodded and said, "Very much so. There's nothing he'd like better than to be the discoverer of the missing egg, which I will let him do, once we learn its secret."

26

DEE & FRIENDS - SLIPPING THROUGH THE ALLEY

They made their way to the postal center where Dee and Jamal waited outside while Dimitri retrieved the key. Then they walked to the house.

"You guys have a coffee in the café while I check it out," said Dimitri.

He returned a few minutes later and sat down to a coffee with them.

"Lots of dust, it doesn't appear that anyone has been inside for quite some time. I guess they don't care as long as I pay."

"We heading there now or do we need anything else?" asked Jamal.

"We'd better eat. I don't want to bring any food into the rental, and I hope we aren't there for long."

They ate quickly and quietly. Dimitri spoke as they finished, "The unit is down the block, third one on the left. The name on the buzzer Is Khrushchev."

"Really," said Dee. "How original."

"No one would bother me on the off chance I'm related. Anyway, I'll go first. Give me a few minutes then come over one at a time. Ring the buzzer, I'll let you inside. Third floor, walk up."

"Convenient and accessible," said Jamal slyly.

"Nobody else wanted it, and it was cheap."

They followed Dimitri's directions and a short time later all three were holed up in the unit. It had an old battered kitchen table with a couple of chairs, a broken down couch, and one double bed.

"I'll take the couch, you guys can share the bed," said Dimitri.

Dee and Jamal both looked at him. "You guys know each other, plus I'll be going out later tonight, after dark, to visit my friend. I don't want to wake you."

They sat around making small talk for a couple of hours until the night was well settled.

"It's about time for me to go. I don't know how long I'll be. Don't answer the pager for anyone but me. I'll give you two short beeps and a long one."

"You're not going to tell us his name?" asked Jamal.

"You'll meet him soon enough and, until then, its better you don't know." He waved and slipped out the door.

"He's cautious," said Jamal.

"I guess he's had to be," replied Dee.

———

They talked for a short time and then decided to lie down.

"You think they're in the Maldives by now?" asked Jamal.

"They should have gotten there a few hours ago," replied Dee.

"Must be nice. I wish I could check in with them."

"Yeah, but Dmitri told us no communications after we left the longship. Not until we're safely out of the country."

"It's hard to believe the Russians have such a complete blanket on all communications."

"It is, but our country probably has one too. We just don't hear about it."

27

DEE & FRIENDS - INTO THE NIGHT

They had been sleeping for a couple of hours when they heard the buzzer, two short and one long. Then a moment of silence and two short and one long. Dee got out of the bed and went to the speaker.

He pressed the button and said, "Da?"

"Very funny," came the reply.

Recognizing Dimitri, Dee hit the buzzer and sat on the couch arm waiting for him to arrive. A few moments later he heard footsteps on the stairs and then a knock at the door. Dee stepped across, stood beside the door, and grunted again.

"It's me."

Dee opened the door and allowed Dimitri inside before closing the door behind him. Jamal had wandered in from the bedroom. He and Dee sat in the two kitchen chairs while Dimitri sprawled on the couch.

"It was good to see him and he's happy to help. Excited actually, quite excited when I told him about the egg."

"Did you tell him about the room?" asked Jamal.

"I held that one back. Some leverage perhaps, and it'll be easier to show him what you think than to try and explain it."

"What happens next?" asked Dee.

"He's going to send a van over in the morning. Actually, it'll look like it's out on errands and one of those will be to pick us up and take us to their processing area. Out of sight of the tourists and the security."

"What will he do?" asked Jamal.

"I just told him it was a nesting egg, and that there was a message inside that he would need to look at. That it didn't mean anything to me."

"Didn't he want to know what it said?" asked Jamal.

"Yes, but I kept him in suspense. I didn't need him poking around on the computer trying to get a jump on deciphering. Best he know a little at a time."

"You mean like us?" said Dee.

"Exactly. Let's get some sleep."

———

THEY HAD ONLY BEEN LYING DOWN FOR A FEW MOMENTS WHEN there was a great crashing noise at the door. Dee and Jamal bolted upright. The bed did not have a view into the living room. They eased to both sides of the opening and listened. It was Novak and another man.

"Dimitri, did you really think you could hide from me? We've known about this little place almost from the beginning. The landlord phoned it in to us. You paying him all these years has been the easiest money of his life. I know he hates that it's over."

"How did you know?"

"Sergei ran across your name from some of the other security services. They suspected you were a double agent. He recognized the last name and thought you might be related to the priest. He put a tail on you. It was simple. And by the way, the freight hauler, the driver, he called it in too. He said three men arrived on a transport plane and caught a ride. It looked suspicious, and he wanted to do his duty. So we backtracked from him to the pilot. Terrible thing about that, the pilot broke his arm while we were having a conversation about you."

"There was no need to hurt him."

"He did it to himself, aiding an enemy of the state: you!"

"I'm a loyal Russian."

"Yes, and I'm the czar's grandson. Now, let's get moving. By the way, where are the other two?"

Dimitri got up off the couch, which he had unfolded the night before. There wasn't much space. He pointed toward the bedroom and stepped beside the second man who stood behind Novak.

Novak took a step toward the bedroom. "Gentlemen," he called out, just before he stepped through the opening.

Dee and Jamal stood against the wall, one on either side of the opening. Each of them held a kitchen chair they had moved into the room the night before when Dimitri had unfolded the couch.

Novak took his first step into the room, and simultaneously Dee and Jamal swung their chairs. Dee went high and Jamal went low. Dee's chair caught Novak in the face and the upper chest. Jamal's caught him in the stomach and groin. He went down with a muffled groan and collapsed on the floor.

Back in the living room, Dimitri drove his elbow into the back of the second man's neck, who slumped forward and fell over Novak.

"Well done, gentlemen," said Dimitri.

"We were just hoping you had a plan for the second guy," said Jamal.

"Let's secure them before they come to," replied Dimitri.

They pulled each of the men further into the bedroom and sat them in the up-righted chairs.

"Good thing those were sturdy," said Jamal. "I imagined them breaking into kindling."

"Russians make sturdy furniture. Not always attractive in the Soviet style, but very solid."

Dimitri pulled a knife from his pocket and cut the venetian blind cords to secure the men's wrists. "Check them for weapons and phones or other communication, also car keys."

They pulled Makarov pistols and knives from each man, along with a leather sap and brass knuckles from the second man, also cell phones and a pager. "We'll dispose of most of that stuff on the way out. They probably have tracers in their shoes, belts, or watches. Grab those as well."

Dimitri laced each man's hands at the wrists. He pulled their arms behind the chair back and cinched them as tight as possible.

"Cut some more cord from the blinds, we'll need to tie their feet to the chairs as well."

Dee and Jamal each cut additional lengths. They let Dimitri tie the men up.

"Okay, we also need to gag them."

"That's easy for this one," said Jamal as he pointed at the second man. "We can use his tie."

Dimitri grabbed it, pulling it off the man's neck and quickly wrapping it around his head after stuffing a third of it into his mouth.

"I hope he can breathe through his nose. That polyester is going to be tasty," added Jamal.

Dee rolled his eyes and pointed to Novak. "What about him?"

Dimitri looked down at Novak's feet. "You got his shoes, pull his socks."

Dee grabbed one and Jamal the other. They handed them to Dimitri.

Dimitri knotted them together and then stretched them

across Novak's mouth, around his head and tied it off in the back. Then he tied a leg from each one of the chairs together.

"Good thing the socks were nylon," said Jamal.

Dee looked at him oddly.

"They stretch well."

"Okay you two clowns, grab the stuff and let's go."

"What about our ride?" said Dee.

"Plans change."

28

DEE & FRIENDS - ON THE MOVE

They hustled down the steps, and Dimitri stopped them at the door. "Let me take a quick look to see if they had any backup."

He peered out the window in each direction. "I see their vehicle but no one else. Of course, they could be down the block. Let me go get in the car and see if anyone else pops up. I'll signal you to come out. It's the black Mercedes sedan in the sea of Ladas."

Dimitri stepped out the door, looked up and down the street and proceeded slowly toward the Mercedes. He got inside and started the car. Sitting there for several seconds, he finally waved at them and held up one finger. Jamal went first then Dee.

Dimitri slid the car into traffic and they were off.

"We seem to be going out of town?" said Dee.

"We are," replied Dimitri. "It's a misdirection. There's a park by the river up ahead. We'll dispose of the non-essential trackable things in the water. Each of you keep one of the guns and knives, but split up the sap and the brass knuckles. I had wanted to keep the impression of you as civilians. But now, after the attack on Novak, you are most certainly wanted and he will kill you if he can, better to be armed."

"Can I ask you something?" said Dee.

"Certainly."

"Why didn't you kill him?"

Dimitri was silent for a moment. "Killing a Russian state security man, especially a high ranking one, is a very serious crime. As far as I know, at the moment, I only have Novak after me. If it got reported that I killed him the entire service would be alerted. There'd be no escaping for any of us. We're close, with the egg and the room. I need to see it through. If you hadn't been there, I might have thought more about it. But I'm an Intelligence officer, not a field operative. I've shot several men and killed a couple. I still remember those moments distinctly. I don't want to add to them."

They rode in silence for a few moments.

"Are we safe to keep the car?" asked Jamal.

"I've been thinking about that. I'm sure it has trackers on it as well. It's probably best to dump it. I'll get us onto a main road near a bus stop. We'll park it and walk away. Take the bus to the museum."

"Where can we hold out until the museum opens?" asked Dee.

"It's a big facility and I've spent a great deal of time in and around it with my friend. There are several locations where we can remain unobserved until he arrives."

Dimitri pulled the car into a surface parking lot and switched it off. They got out, and he pocketed the keys. "Let's go catch the bus."

There were two young teenage boys walking toward them, despite the time of night. Dee and Jamal both tensed. Dimitri reached into his pocket and pulled out the car keys. A few feet from the boys he tossed them. "It's in the surface lot." The boys looked at him for a moment, grins appearing on their faces, and then they rushed past the men toward the car.

"No telling where it will end up," said Jamal.

"That's the plan."

————

THEY RODE FOR SEVERAL MINUTES. DIMITRI LEANED BACK against the seat and closed his eyes. "Rest for a minute while you can. It'll get busy later today."

Half an hour later Dimitri opened his eyes. "The museum is just up ahead. We'll stay on the bus until right before it crosses the Winter Canal. The stop there leads to a small alley we can duck into. It will take us to the back of the theater and out of sight. We'll slip inside when the doors open."

————

NOVAK SLOWLY WORKED HIS SWOLLEN EYES OPEN. SOMETHING had hit him across the face. He gagged, what was that taste. Shrugging his shoulders he realized where he was and that he was tied securely in an old wooden chair. His assistant was still passed out and tied in the chair beside him. Novak tried to jiggle his chair and realized that both chairs were tied together. He looked down and realized his socks, shoes, and belt were missing.

Dimitri has done this, with the help of the two men. I'll kill them all, after he tells me what he knows about the egg. He can't hide. I'm done wasting time on him.

It's going to be difficult for my men to track me. Maybe the car. I bet he took that too. Novak tried to wiggle his legs but couldn't. *I bet he took everything. How long will we have to sit here?*

————

THE LINES HAD FORMED AN HOUR EARLIER FOR ADMITTANCE TO the museum and at the appointed hour the crowds slowly began to move forward and inside.

The three men slipped inside the theater doors. Dimitri pulled a cell phone from his pocket and sent a short text.

"I thought communications were a no-no?" said Jamal.

"They are. Alexi gave me this phone last night. It belongs to the museum. I only sent him a code, easily deniable, if anyone should ever see it or check it."

Dimitri's phone chimed, and he took a quick glance. Then he replied.

"What are you saying this time?" asked Jamal.

"It's a lovely day for the theater," replied Dimitri. "He'll come for us."

They were standing in a small area backstage behind several sets of curtains. A few minutes passed. "Has anyone seen Dimitri?" a voice announced.

To which Dimitri replied, "Why yes, he's just over here."

A moment later a slender late-middle aged man with dark hair and dark eyes came between the curtains. He stood very still as he acknowledged Dimitri with a nod.

Dimitri stepped forward. "Alexi, this is Dee and Jamal. They have been helping me and were instrumental in locating the egg."

Alexi's cool exterior relaxed a little, and he quickly shook both men's hands. "Dimitri has been looking for so long. I want to hear all about it, but let's get you to my office."

He motioned them in a close circle. "Because of certain circumstances in my life, I fear my communications are wired."

Alexi looked up at Dimitri, who replied, "I told them." Alexi nodded in return.

"Because of my wife's position, or positions I should say, I believe that my office has ears, but it is the most secure location that I can place you. When we arrive, I'll turn on some music.

We must communicate by writing. There is no evidence of a camera, only sound. Put your thoughts on paper, slip it to me, I'll read it, and shred it. Anything I hand you to read, hand back to me after, and I'll do the same."

With that he turned and led them out of the curtains. "Walk behind me casually, a few feet back, just make the same turns I do."

29

DEE & FRIENDS - A DAY AT THE OFFICE

They arrived at his office without incident. There was a small conference table with four chairs. Alexi directed them to sit. There were pads of paper and pens on the table. The shredder was against the wall beside Alexi.

"This looks like a common theme," said Dee.

"I'm afraid it is," replied Alexi. Then he wrote, "Even when one is just speculating or letting off steam, it's best to be discreet."

He continued with another note. "How can I help? Can I see the egg?" He shoved it to the middle of the table.

Dee and Jamal looked to Dimitri, who pushed the pad back to Alexi, who took the sheet of paper and slipped it into the micro-shredder. What had been a piece of paper was now a palm full of dust.

Dimitri wrote the following and pushed it to Alexi. "For now, let me ask how you are prepared to help. Until you actually participate, you can deny participation and say you were forced."

Alexi smiled, took the paper and shredded it.

"Whatever you need."

"Can you examine the other egg? Can we remove it from display for a short time?"

"Yes, of course. It needs to be cleaned and the case wiped down from time to time. That's easy, we put up a sign. The display is closed for a few hours or whatever you need."

"Let's start with that."

Alexi nodded and picked up a phone from the center of the table. He gave a few short commands in Russian and returned the phone to its cradle.

"It's on its way here."

"We'd like to examine it briefly, in your presence of course, for certain design elements."

Alexi was rubbing his hands together clearly in anticipation. "I can't wait."

"Neither can I."

A few minutes later there was a knock on the door, and Alexi rose to answer. He returned shortly with a small wooden box lined with straw and the egg.

"Looks familiar, doesn't it?" said Dimitri.

Alexi pointed to the pad. Dimitri nodded. Then he took the egg in his hands and slowly turned it around. When he completed the circle, he handed it to Jamal and nodded.

Jamal looked to Dee, who nodded in return. Jamal sat the egg down and quickly wrote on the pad, then he pushed it to Alexi. "Dee found the other one."

Alexi nodded at all three men and then specifically to Dee.

Jamal picked the egg up again and slowly turned it around while sliding his fingers along the surface. His fingers stopped, and he smiled.

He turned to Alexi and wrote on the pad, "Okay to manipulate the egg? Like we did the other one?"

Alexi looked confused for a moment and then turned to Dimitri, who nodded.

Alexi nodded to Jamal and leaned forward in his chair to watch.

Jamal torqued the egg softly, left to right, then right to left. Then he pulled up from the top and down from the bottom. Then he torqued it again. He repeated this cycle several times. Then, all at once, the egg slipped apart and revealed the next smaller one inside.

Alexi nearly fell from his chair, his eyes wide.

Dimitri wrote a quick note. "Has anyone ever examined the egg?"

Alexi replied, "Not since I've been here and never to the best of my knowledge. Most of the party leaders have always been afraid to touch it."

Jamal had begun working on the smaller egg. Alexi saw this and quickly wrote on the pad, "Nesting dolls?"

The three other men nodded.

"How deep?"

"Wait and see."

Jamal slowly separated the second egg and laid it aside as he took out the third egg.

Alexi leaned back in his chair, amazement on his face. He quickly scribbled on the pad, "How in the world did you find it?"

Dimitri replied, "One thing at a time. There's more to see."

Jamal got the third egg apart and was now circling the fourth egg with his fingers. Again, it was about the size of a chicken egg.

Alexi had to ask, "How much smaller can it go?"

Jamal held up a finger, as if to say, wait a minute, and then he found the star shape on the top of the egg and depressed. The egg popped open and there was another piece of scroll.

The three other men sat motionless.

Jamal lowered the egg and withdrew the scroll. He unrolled it and held it open with both hands. Then he let it roll back up and put it back in the egg. He wrote on the pad, "It says, 'it never left'. In the same gold script as the other egg." Then he handed the small egg and the scroll to Dimitri.

Dimitri set the egg down and took the scroll out to read. He held it for several seconds and then slowly shook his head. Taking the pad he wrote, "Does that phrase mean anything to you," and slid it to Alexi. Dimitri then handed the egg and the scroll to Dee.

Alexi read the message and then reread it. He looked up at Dimitri and shook his head.

Dee handed the egg and the scroll to Alexi, who grabbed it quickly and spread the scroll out. He looked at it for several seconds before setting it down. Then he wrote, "I have no idea what that means or what substance it's written with."

Dimitri took the pad and scribbled a note he slid to Alexi. "The other egg had a similar scroll and writing, in the same gold color and substance, and it said, 'in the other egg'."

Alexi replied, "What could all that mean? I never expected that you would find the egg and, if you did it was just going to be a Fabergé egg, a priceless Fabergé egg, but none the less, just an egg."

"I didn't know what to expect, if I ever found it. I have to give these two credit." He pointed at Dee and Jamal.

"How did they do it?"

"Do you really want to know? Are you prepared for the possible consequences?"

"Like what? I don't know what you mean, but of course I want to know."

"They were actually on a different quest, looking at murals in some of the oldest churches for clues about a gold room that appeared to be inside the Winter Palace."

At that Alexi drew back and paused, but then quickly shredded the paper with the note.

"There was the Amber Room, which was moved to the

Catherine Palace and stolen by the Nazis during World War II. It has never been recovered. Could what they were looking for have been old enough to predate the move?"

"When did the room move?"

"1755."

"Not likely, their clues seemed to revolve around Nicholas II, last heard from in 1918."

"His reign was from 1894 until 1917."

"Still not far enough back."

"I have no idea."

"Let Jamal put the egg back together and you get it back on display before there are any questions. Then we'll go from there."

"There's more?"

Dimitri smiled at Alexi.

Jamal had begun reassembling the egg, including the scroll. It wasn't like any of them were going to forget the message. Alexi placed the assembled egg back in the box and after a brief phone call, carried it to the door to be resettled in the exhibit.

"Can you get around inside this place at night?" asked Dimitri on the pad.

Alexi nodded and wrote, "Yes. I'll need to make arrangements. What are we doing and where?"

Dimitri pointed to Dee who took the pad and wrote, "In the War Memorial Hall, Armorial Hall, and possibly the Small Throne Room."

Alexi looked at him, nodded and shrugged.

Dimitri then wrote, "Where can we hole up and spend the day?"

Alexi thought for a moment, then replied, "Probably safest here. I can work in the ante-chamber, order you some food, and run any interference needed. Just be sure and don't talk. Use the pad."

30

DEE & FRIENDS - THE HUNT CONTINUES

Novak's assistant finally came around. He muttered in a groggy state, the sound mangled by his tie. Novak snapped at him through the sock, "Wake up!"

The man shook his head and muttered.

"Look, we're tied together," Novak mumbled. "We need to work together. Let's try to rattle the chair and bang the floor. Maybe the noise will get someone's attention," said Novak.

The man mumbled something.

"No, they won't be able to track us. Dimitri took everything."

The man looked at himself and noticed his missing clothing. He began to thrash in the seat and Novak joined him as best he could. Their feet were securely tied to the chair legs and just barely reached the floors. Plus, they were barefooted and trying not to land on their toes.

They bounced around for what seemed like hours and then they heard a sound. The door being unlocked. A moment later the landlord, the man who had called Novak, walked in the room. He hurriedly went to remove their gags.

Novak spit out the taste of the sock. "Hurry and get a knife. You'll never get these knots untied."

The landlord scurried away and returned shortly with another man. Each of them had a knife and began working on the bindings.

Once freed, Novak stood and stretched his muscles. "Did you hear us?" he asked the landlord.

The man shook his head. "I saw all of you, them and then you, go inside. I never saw anyone come out. When I got closer to the door, I heard the sounds."

"If I'm successful in killing those men, you will be rewarded."

The man nodded nervously.

Novak turned to his assistant. "Let's go."

———

Dee, Jamal and Dimitri passed the remainder of the morning away speculating and passing notes back and forth. Alexi ordered some lunch, and they attacked it hungrily.

"How do we go about looking for the room?" asked Jamal. "I mean I know where to go, but how do we approach Alexi?"

"I think we just take him to where you fell and show him what you saw. He's going to know more about the building than anyone else, isn't he?" said Dee.

"He should and I believe he does," replied Dimitri. "I think at this point he'll believe us or at least feel like we are credible. I'm just not sure how he can go about disrupting the various rooms. The palace and museum are serious business to the state."

They heard footsteps and voices coming toward them.

"Hurry, you must go. Novak and his men are coming," whispered Alexi. "Follow me." He led them out of his office and through the back door of the outer room.

"My office is near the corner of the original Hermitage, off the Winter Canal. Turn left at the end of the hall and you'll be in the western loggia. Follow it until you reach the crossover to the Winter Palace. You'll be in a small ante-room and then in the Great Throne Room. Exit there into the War Memorial and the Armorial Hall. You know those areas. There are lots of tourists. It will make it difficult for Novak to cause a scene. After that you're on your own. If you make it back tonight, we'll look at whatever else you had to show me."

Dimitri, Jamal, and Dee hurried down the hall toward the loggia.

"This is why you didn't tell Alexi more, isn't it?" asked Dee, as they scrambled down the corridor.

Dimitri nodded while taking a quick look back. "I don't think Novak will question Alexi more than generally. He is aware of Alexi's connections. He may in fact know Mrs. Alexi, Maria."

"I thought that was a French name?" said Jamal.

"It is, but it's also Russian. Her father was a Russian diplomat, and her mother was a French dancer. They settled on the name Maria."

"How do you know all that?" asked Jamal.

"We were all once friends, long ago. When we get inside the Great Throne room, move quickly but don't run. It'll be too easy for any of Novak's men that are on duty to spot us on the cameras. Stay a few feet apart with other people in between, but do not lose sight of one another."

"Should we head for the Jordan stairway and try to get outside?" asked Dee.

"That's probably a good strategy. If Novak has men on duty, plus what he has with him, it'll be too easy to pin us down, once they locate us with the cameras. That's inevitable inside. If we can get out into the streets, we can better hide."

They crossed quickly into the War Memorial and then the Armorial Hall.

"This is where we wanted to be," said Jamal.

"Yeah, just not like this," replied Dimitri. "Separate a little more."

They continued quickly from the Hall to the Small Throne Room and toward the stairway. The crowds were thick, and the men had to work to maintain their pace against the tightly packed crowds flowing in the opposite direction.

Crossing the corridor before turning for the staircase, Dee and Jamal were several feet apart and watching Dimitri's back. He was leading the way when he suddenly froze and stopped. He turned quickly and began to flow with the crowd toward Dee and Jamal, who were frozen in place.

As Dimitri reached them, he whispered, "Come along. Novak's men are coming up the stairs. I saw them on the landing just below."

They flowed along with the crowd and back toward the Small Throne Room. A group of tourists stopped in front of them, and a short heavyset woman began to drone on about the room. Each man blended into a section of the group so that they could see in each direction. As the group collapsed behind the guide to move to the next stop, Dimitri whispered to Jamal, who was closest to him, "We need to try and get to the souvenir shop to change what we look like."

Dimitri stayed with the group until they stopped in the Armorial Hall. Waving to Dee and Jamal, Dimitri kept going toward the far end of the room.

As they caught up to him, he whispered, "We'll go down the back stairs here and into the gift shop. Find something to disguise yourself and head out that door toward the Square."

They descended the steps and swung into the gift shop. It was crowded. Dimitri worked his way to the back wall where there were tee shirts, sweatshirts, jackets, and hats.

"Pick something out that's not too obnoxious." He grabbed a blue cap and a blue jacket. Jamal went with red, Dee with black.

Outside, they put them on and started across the Square, three tourists taking in the sights. "Look for a group and mingle. Stay with them until we get out of the Square. We'll catch a cab and disappear."

31

DEE & FRIENDS - SQUARED AWAY

Novak was not happy. He'd seen the three men on the camera, but his men had lost them in the crowd. Now he was in Alexi's office.

He sat down opposite Alexi. "I have questions."

"Go ahead."

"Did you know those men were here?" he said, pointing to a screen grab of the three of them in the Small Throne Room.

"No, who are they?"

"One of them is Dimitri Kuznetsov, whom I believe you know."

Alexi leaned forward toward Novak's phone. "Yes, I knew him. It's been some time since I've seen him. I didn't recognize him in that picture."

"It is a bit blurred."

"What is the problem?"

"That doesn't concern you directly. Do you have any idea why he'd be here?"

"None whatsoever. Who's that with him?"

"Not important, it's all a state matter. We need Dimitri. Put your staff on alert."

"Certainly."

Novak sat back in the chair. This was where he normally got persuasive if he had any idea or even a feeling that something wasn't right, or accurate, or truthful. *But Alexi had a direct pipeline into the Politburo.* Not one Novak would want to have, not in that fashion. Novak actually knew Mrs. Alexi or 'Missy' as she was often called. *He needed to be aware of her influence just the same.*

"So you will inform me if any of these three men are seen on the premises again?"

"As best we can from your screenshot."

That was the thing. Alexi didn't have the proper attitude either. Perhaps there was something to be done about that after the Dimitri issue was resolved.

Novak rose, nodded, and left the office to return to his men.

———

THEY FOLLOWED A GROUP OF SENIOR CITIZENS FROM ONE OF the river cruises until they departed the Square for their bus. Slipping away, the men hurried down the street and into a café.

"We need to figure out what to do," said Dimitri.

"What? You mean we can't go back to your spy house?" kidded Dee.

"Ignore him," added Jamal.

Dimitri sighed and said in a tense voice, "It's been a long day."

"Yes it has," said Dee. "And I have a plan. Humor me for just a few minutes." He pointed out the window, "There, let's grab that cab."

They exited quickly and flagged the cab. Getting in beside the driver, while Dimitri and Jamal got in the back, Dee said, "Lotte Hotel."

"On the Moyka River?" asked the driver.

Dee nodded and leaned back in the seat.

Dimitri leaned forward. "How do you know this place. It's very upscale."

"We stayed there when we first came to town, before the cruise."

The cab arrived in only a couple of minutes. Dee tipped the man, and they all got out.

"Follow me," he said.

Entering the lobby Dee waved to the desk clerk, who replied,. "Mr. Sanders, good to see you again."

"Good to be here. Would you have a suite available?"

The clerk paused for a moment, checking his records. "Yes, we do."

"Can I request it for three nights with three keys?"

"Certainly."

———

Several moments later they were inside the suite and exploring its contents.

"Very nice," said Dimitri. "You stay in places like this often?"

"When spy houses aren't available," replied Dee.

"You're not going to let me forget that are you?"

"It was quite the adventure."

"So now we're going to hide in plain sight."

"Something like that. Novak will expect us to be on the run because he's thinking of what you would do. He's paid no attention to Jamal and me."

"Mr. Sanders, you would make a good spy. So would you Mr. Jones. Not once has either of you panicked, and there have been multiple opportunities for you to do so."

"We've been traveling for the better part of the last year, and we've had a few close encounters."

"Learning under pressure, huh, that's not a bad thing."

"We try to pay attention," added Jamal.

"Let me say, well done. You never know what you might need to know."

"Speaking of, why don't you lead the way for us to find some new clothes and maybe a good steak? We could use a different look, ditch these tourist duds."

"Happy to. How about a brief introduction to some good Russian vodka and maybe a short nap before the evening's festivities?"

"A nap?" said Jamal.

Dimitri held up his phone. "I still have this from the museum. Let me see what I can do about tonight's entertainment." He punched in a number and texted a "?".

In only a few seconds, his phone chimed, and he held up a message which he read to them. "Show starts at 10:30pm."

Dee and Jamal both looked at him questioningly.

"Alexi will meet us at the rear doors of the Imperial Theater at 10:30pm and we'll go have a look at what you have to show him."

"What about Novak?" asked Dee.

"Like you said, he'll be beating the streets. Looking for me, or for us."

32

DEE & FRIENDS - THE SHOW MUST GO ON

They approached the rear doors of the theater and Dimitri knocked twice quickly and then once longer.

"What is that knock pattern?" asked Jamal.

"It's an 'A' in Morse code," replied Dimitri. "Really just a confirmation."

They heard the same knock returned to them and then the door opened and there stood Alexi.

"I see you survived and avoided our friend, Novak," said Alexi.

Dimitri grinned at him. "My new friends," he said pointing at Dee and Jamal, "are quite adept. I've enjoyed working with them."

"Shall we get underway? While we have the opportunity," said Alexi.

"War Memorial and Armorial Hall," said Jamal. "I want to show you something I saw…"

"And then share something we found," concluded Dee.

Alexi led the way. It took a couple of minutes as they were at the far end of the Hermitage and had to cross over to the Winter Palace.

They reached the entrance of the War Memorial and Jamal led the way to the end of the room, near the painting of Alexander I on his stallion.

"I fell here, slick shoes, and when I did, looking up at the ceiling I noticed that the corners of the room didn't make a square ninety-degree angle. Instead, they came in and then went back to the other wall."

"As if there was some other space beyond," said Alexi.

"Yes, and if we go into the Armorial Hall to this end, I think we will see the same thing."

"Let's go look."

They did, and the ceiling was in the same arrangement.

"Don't know what to make of that," said Alexi. "It is odd. The rooms should be square."

"There's more," said Dee. "We saw a painting in the loggia, and I can show it to you, that did not seem to belong. It was not a reproduction of any at the Vatican, as specified, but a rendering of the Winter Palace, next to a second rendering of a local church."

"That is odd. I'm surprised I've never noticed," said Alexi.

"It's on the side of one of the columns. It's not very prominent and if Jamal and I hadn't stopped right beside it, we probably never would have noticed."

"So what does that mean?" asked Alexi.

"Nothing in and of itself. But it led us to look for the church that seemed to be a clue. We did, and that led us to other churches with more paintings. Slowly a picture of a gold room emerged and then it was revealed to be inside the Winter Palace. We had just toured here and were not aware of any such room. It all just seemed very odd and we probably wouldn't have done anything about it, until we ran into Dimitri."

"I saw them looking at paintings and pursuing something. I

began to follow them. We met in Yaroslavl Park, along with some of Novak's men that I ran off, and then we joined forces. I helped them look for the paintings and they helped me try to figure out or locate the egg. Ultimately, they seemed to be linked together."

"That's unbelievable," replied Alexi. "But, I have a piece of news too. I had one of the museum technicians research a partial picture I took of the message inside the egg, just a single word. I didn't tell him where it was from. I just asked him to determine the medium of the writing. He came back a couple of hours later and said it was liquid amber that had hardened. I thanked him and went on my way. But you now have my curiosity highly aroused."

"I have a request," said Dimitri. "Here in the Armorial Hall, behind that painting in the corner, would you allow me to drill a hole in the wall and take a look?"

"You can drill a hole small enough to look inside, if there is anything?" said Alexi.

"I can't see but my borescope or snake camera can." Dimitri pulled a three-foot cable with a lens on one end and an eyepiece on the other. "Would your men have a small bore drill?"

Alexi rubbed his chin. "Behind the painting, minimal mess?"

"Yes."

"Give me a minute and I'll get it from the maintenance room." Alexi stepped away.

"He's really going to let us do this?" asked Jamal.

"I think he's seen enough to assign you some credibility. Plus, this could be huge and work in his favor. His immediate concern will be keeping it low profile so there's no evidence of activity or damage, so as not to arouse suspicion or unwanted intrusion."

Alexi reappeared with a drill, a masonry bit, and an extension for the bit. "Let me drill the hole."

Dimitri nodded and Jamal and Dee stepped to each side of the painting and removed it from the wall. They sat it against the adjacent wall.

Alexi shook his head and then quickly ran the bit through the wall and retracted it.

"Thick walls, huh," said Dimitri.

"Built to last," replied Alexi.

Dimitri assembled the camera and eased the head into the wall. "Good thing I got plenty of cable." He pushed for several seconds and then felt no more resistance. Dimitri turned on the camera and watched the screen. There wasn't much light from the lens, but Dimitri could definitely see what looked like a wall covered in something golden. Each of the other men took a quick look over his shoulder.

He then spun the camera lens in the other direction and there seemed to be more of the gold wall.

"Whatever it is, there seems to be a good bit of it," said Dimitri.

Alexi sighed. "Yeah, definitely worth a look. It's going to be messy."

"No place there could be a hidden door?" asked Dee.

"Doubtful. Possible, but not likely. The palace has been remodeled, refurbished, there was a fire in the 1830s and there was a lot of rebuilding. If there was one, I'm guessing it was covered up or closed off. I've never heard of one, not even a rumor or gossip or a legend."

"What can you do?" asked Dimitri.

"Let me think about it overnight. There's nothing we can do until tomorrow anyway. I can't just go tearing into the wall. It'll have to be organized. Something specific." He glanced up at the ceiling and then pointed. "Up there, you know I swear we might have some water damage. I can partition this corner off and remediate. I have a couple of workmen who I think can handle it discreetly. Would that work?"

Dimitri was grinning.

"First thing in the morning, get back here and I'll get it underway."

33

DEE & FRIENDS - PROSPECTING

Although they were tired, there wasn't much sleep that night. Dimitri was particularly jumpy and nervous.

"It's been over a hundred years since Anastasia took the pearl, over seventy years since my grandfather last touched it, and who knows how long since this room was last seen or remembered."

"Yeah, it's a lot to take in," said Jamal.

"Won't be long now, better get some rest," added Dee.

Dimitri just couldn't seem to do it and paced around the living area portion of the suite for most of the night.

After restraining Dimitri for as long as they could, all three men made their way to the Winter Palace the following morning. Reaching the Armorial Hall, they saw a canopied area in the corner where the painting had hung.

As they made their way toward it, they could see signs asking patrons to step around the obstruction and apologizing for the inconvenience. As they neared and a guard began to step toward them, Alexi emerged from inside the canopy.

He raised a hand to halt the guard and spoke to the men.

"I've been expecting you for a while. In fact, I figured you'd be here first thing this morning."

"That would have been my preference," said Dimitri.

"We thought you'd probably need some time to get started," said Jamal.

"Thanks. That was helpful to gather the crew and the supplies we needed. What I'm wondering about now is, we are most of the way through the wall. I don't want to damage what's on the inside. We've slowed down on the premise that the interior wall could be quite valuable, and we don't want to damage it."

"Can you work through to the backing?" asked Dee.

"That's what we're attempting. It's mostly stone that we have to cut out in small slabs as we get closer to the thickness of the wall."

"Dimitri, do you still have your snake camera?" asked Dee.

"Yes," he replied.

Looking at Alexi, Dee said, "Could we have Dimitri take another look and see if he can determine what sort of backing there is on the wall?"

"Great idea, come inside and let me halt the workers."

Dee, Jamal, and Dimitri followed Alexi under the canopy and up to the wall where two men were working.

Alexi held up a hand. "Hold on men, let Dimitri take a peek, maybe make it easier for you."

Both men nodded and stepped back.

Dimitri ran the cable through what remained of the wall, which was only about six inches. He swiveled the camera in several directions and his face took on a look of excitement.

"It's brighter in the daylight. I'm not sure what the light source is, but it's better than last night. It's a room, maybe twelve by ten or twelve by twelve. I can't quite see it all. But whatever it is looks spectacular. It's assembled pieces of something making various designs and patterns. It's quite unique. Here take a look."

Dee and Jamal pointed to Alexi, who went first and came away shaking his head. Jamal followed and then Dee.

"It's stunning, whatever it is," said Jamal.

Dee looked to Dimitri, who was clearly excited. "Can you pull the camera back into the wall and see what is holding the material in place?"

"I certainly can try."

Dmitri worked the cable slowly back and forth until he found the necessary depth and then he turned the lens from left to right repeatedly.

"I think there's a wood backing. The material is adhered to the wood, and the wood is attached to the wall. The wood is probably an inch thick, which would indicate the gold material has some weight."

"Can you tell how much stone is left?" asked Dee.

Dimitri went back to work. "Couple of inches at best. You're getting close."

Alexi looked at his workmen. "Can you tell by feel when the wall material density changes?"

"Somewhat. It helps to know we're only about two inches out. We'll set the next cut for that depth and see what is left." They started to work.

"Shouldn't be long," said Alexi.

They watched as the workmen cut away the stone. As they extracted it, there was an uncut remainder which began to crumble as they cleared away the cut debris.

"It's going to be like deconstructing a puzzle," said Alexi. "We don't know the sizes of the wood backing. We're going to need to make the hole larger."

The workmen had cut a foot square hole.

"Can they enlarge it to two feet square?" asked Dee.

"Surely that would be enough to get an idea of the size of the pieces of wood backing."

Alexi nodded, and the men went to work.

Alexi led Dimitri and the others outside the canopy where it was a little quieter.

"It shouldn't take them long," said Alexi.

"What do you think we are going to find?" asked Dimitri.

"It looks a lot like amber, which makes no sense. The Amber Room was moved to the Catherine Palace in 1755. It was relocated there and expanded by Rastrelli, the Italian architect. Then it was stolen by the Nazis in WWII and never recovered, thought to be destroyed in a bombing or a subsequent fire."

"Could some portion of it or a different one have been retained?" asked Dee.

"It's a documented fact that it was moved. Many people saw it afterwards. The original was gifted by Frederick I of Prussia to Peter the Great to solidify their partnership in a war against Sweden. Empress Elizabeth ordered it to be moved from the Winter Palace to the Catherine Palace."

"What else could it be?" asked Jamal.

"And what about the egg?" added Dimitri. "The message in the 2nd egg says, 'It never left.'"

"That part doesn't make sense. It's almost like the egg predated the move, but the timing is wrong. Nicholas II was the last czar. He was much later in time than when the original room was moved. He had the eggs made for his wife, and presumably the message made for his throne. Something doesn't fit."

"Could it be as simple as they didn't move it?" asked Dee. "They let out the story that it was being moved and enhanced by the Italian, but they retained the original?"

"Why would they do that?" asked Alexi. "They were among the most powerful people in their world."

"Being in 1755, we'll never know for sure, but let's just say they did keep the original room. The royal family would be aware of it, even when no one else was. Maybe it was some palace intrigue or secret negotiation or just to create a distraction. But if they passed the information from czar to czar, by the time it got to Nicholas II, and his wife, Alexandra Feodorovna, who had a sense of imminent danger or impending disaster—they had the eggs made and the message hidden in them so that there would be a clue for any of the surviving family."

"Except that none of the immediate family survived, and the knowledge died with them."

"Which might explain why Anastasia fled with the egg," added Dimitri.

"Yes," replied Alexi. "That would be a plausible explanation. Why else would she take one egg and not both?"

"Even though the egg she took had only a secondary message. And the primary message and egg could have easily disappeared, been stolen, lost in time, anything could have happened to it," said Jamal.

"Maybe she made a mistake when she grabbed it, or the egg was given to her. Even if she'd had the other egg, the meaning of the message was pretty obscure. Anyone finding it would have had to have comprehensive knowledge of the situation," said Dimitri.

"Yes," agreed Alexi. "The information was almost worthless without the family background."

"Most people would have been overwhelmed just by the egg and probably never would have figured out or known that it was nested and that there were three more eggs and a message," said Dee.

"All these years, I never really thought it was anything but an egg," said Dimitri.

"So the paintings were just another set of clues?" asked Jamal.

"It may have been in conjunction with the egg, or it may have been an alternative way to leave clues, or even a backup, if the eggs were lost or not available," replied Alexi.

"The whole thing is unbelievable," added Dimitri.

One of the workmen approached Alexi. "We have the hole finished. There appears to be a seam that we might be able to separate. Come and have a look."

34

DEE & FRIENDS - SECRETS

They followed the workman through the canopy and to the back wall. The opening was now two feet square and there was a seam in the wood backing about a third of the way up from the bottom of the opening.

"Can you get that apart?" asked Alexi.

"I think we can wedge something under the bottom of the upper piece and then push it out at the top. I don't see any type of attachments, like nails or hooks. The pieces must have been glued or whatever type of adhesive they had in that time period."

"Give it a try. Just be careful."

The workman nodded, grinned at Alexi, and turned to his partner. "Get the wedges and a small hammer."

The second man worked two long thin strips underneath the upper piece of wood, holding one in each hand. Then the other man took a small hammer, the size of an upholstery hammer that looked almost like a toy from a child's toolbox, and slowly and softly began to tap the top of the wood. Several taps yielded no movement in the wooden piece.

"I'm going to have to go a little harder," said the workman to Alexi.

Alexi, grim-faced, nodded in return.

The workman swung the hammer harder and there was a slight creak in the wood. He paused for a moment and took another firmer swing. The top of the wooden piece flexed and partially gave way. The man sat the hammer down and, using his bare hand, pushed the top of the piece out while his coworker balanced it on the two metal strips. Turning the piece sideways, the second man brought it through the hole they had just created. He turned to show it to everyone.

Alexi took the piece, turned it over, and ran his fingers across the surface. Then he held it up so the light would shine on it. "Amber. That is definitely amber."

"You think it's a whole room?" asked Dimitri.

"Doesn't make sense, but it looks like it initially." Alexi turned to the workmen. "Can you remove enough pieces that we can get through and into the space?"

"Might take a little time but we should be able to."

"Good, be careful, take the time you need, stack the pieces you remove by that wall. Let me know when you think we can get through."

Alexi led the others back into the Armorial Hall and carefully closed the work curtains behind them.

They started toward his office. He whispered to them as they walked, "It's just unbelievable. There's no precedent or rumor or suggestion of anything like this in any record of the Imperial family."

"So, apparently they could keep a secret?" said Jamal.

"I guess we'll see soon enough," added Dee.

Alexi's phone went off and he looked at the screen as they walked.

"Is that them?" asked Dimitri, "Are they ready?"

"No, something else. Let me send a quick reply," said Alexi.

He tapped the screen for a few moments as they walked toward his office.

—————

Gathered around the conference table, they wrote messages to one another.

"What does this mean for the country?" asked Dimitri.

"It's a great find, an addition to history. The value of the room could be half a billion dollars if this turns out to be the original and can be verified," replied Alexi.

"What about the one that was lost?" asked Dee.

"I expect it was amber and valuable given the time period it was created. I wonder if when Catherine decided to move it, perhaps they couldn't match the original, or maybe the architect had some objection she considered valid."

"And maybe they didn't want anyone to know that," added Dee.

"But why?" asked Jamal.

"At that time the room would certainly have been valuable, but nothing like today," replied Alexi. "For some reason they didn't want to admit what they were doing."

"Or they wanted to keep the original for themselves, for their own enjoyment when they were in the Winter Palace," added Dee.

"Possibly, but we'll probably never know."

There was a knock on the door. Alexi glanced over and the workman was standing outside. He nodded and waved a hand at Alexi.

They all rose and returned to the Armorial Hall.

The opening was large enough that if they stood on a stool they could lean in and work their shoulders though the wall. The plan was hands first and then pulling themselves through with a little assist from their legs. Alexi was the thinnest and shortest. He went first and pushed another small stool in front of him. "When I'm halfway through and my shoulders and hands are clear, I'll set the stool and then use it as resistance to pull my legs through."

Once he was on the other side and standing, he looked back to them. "Let me take a quick look." A few moments later he called out, "It's amazing. I don't doubt this is the original room. The patterns and the workmanship, and it's the correct size of the original. Let me help who's next."

Each of the men worked their way through the wall. When all four were inside, they took up almost half the floor space.

"Twelve by twelve was the original size," said Alexi.

"A door," said Dee. "There has to be a door."

"They might have closed it off," replied Alexi.

"How would they have gotten to it or enjoyed it?"

"Maybe they did want to keep it hidden?"

Dee continued around the room, using the flashlight on his phone and looking at the seams of the various panels. They were arranged like a great puzzle, each piece at a different angle and size, highlighting the amber from every direction. He came to a piece that extended into the room further than the others. "Can we touch this?" he asked as no one had thus far.

"Yes," replied Dimitri. "Just be careful, touch it gently. Remember where you do and we'll wipe it down."

"It's still so bright," said Jamal.

"Probably the low light and the constant temperature in this room," replied Alexi. "Bright sunlight would dry it out, make it brittle, and turn it dull. Amber is basically tree resin. Also, the fact that it hasn't been touched." He looked over his shoulder at Dee.

Dee was studying the prominent piece he had run across but nodded to Alexi. Dee took his shirt and put his hand behind it so that he touched the amber only through the material. There was a distinct click.

Everyone stopped and stood where they were.

There was now a slight break in the wall in front of Dee. It ran from the floor to the ceiling.

"Alexi," said Dee. "I may have found a door. Where would this wall be?"

Alexi turned to him and then relocated himself with the hole they had entered. "You'd be in the corner of the War Memorial Hall near the big painting of Alexander I."

"Near where I fell," said Jamal.

"There's space for me to pull on this door," said Dee. "Do we risk opening it with all the tourists in the museum?"

Alexi looked thoughtful for a moment. "Can you see anything beyond the door?"

Dee pulled it just slightly more open and held his flashlight to it. "It looks wooden."

"There's a head-high chair rail on that wall."

"Secret door?" said Dimitri.

"Let me go look. I'll close the end of the room off for now. I'll text you when I'm ready." Alexi climbed on the stool and worked his way out of the opening. The workmen helped him out. He dusted himself off and said, "Follow me."

35

DEE & FRIENDS - PASSAGEWAY TO THE PAST

Inside the room Dee eased the door further open. There was a wooden wall beyond it. He moved the light around the edges. "Bring your phones over, put more light on it."

Dimitri and Jamal both shone their phones along the perimeter of the door.

On the left side, about halfway down, Jamal noticed a seam in the wood. He pushed it with a finger and the wooden strip hinged open. There was a lever inside. "Look, I think it's a handle," he said and pointed at the spot.

Dimitri and Dee both focused their lights on the opening.

"I bet that if we push that down, it releases a hinge that allows the door to swing open and into the War Memorial Hall," said Dee.

"Should we wait for Alexi?" asked Dimitri.

"Absolutely."

"We might open it up and scare some tourist to death," added Jamal.

They stepped away from the door and resumed looking at the patterns on the walls.

"This is just unbelievable. It must be why the tiles in the

murals were textured. To show how intricate the work is and all the patterns created with the amber," said Jamal.

"I never would have dreamed it while I was looking for the egg. That it would lead to such a discovery," replied Dimitri.

Dee's phone vibrated. He looked down, and the text read, "I'm ready."

He turned and looked at Jamal and Dimitri.

"Let's go see what happens."

The three of them made their way to the opening, and Dee placed a hand on the lever and pulled gently down. It was stiff at first but began to move, and Dee increased the pressure until he heard a small pop. Then he pushed on the wooden frame, and it swung slowly open into the War Memorial Hall. Alexi was standing on the other side with a grin on his face.

"Unbelievable," he said.

All three of the men stepped through and into the hallway.

"Look," said Alexi. "See how it fits into the molding. No one would ever know there was a door there. It's perfect." He handed out flashlights. "For when we go back inside."

"There has to be a release on this side too," said Dee and the men fanned out on each side of the door. "Check the molding on each side of the opening, like what the door was behind."

"Here," said Dimitri. He stood to the right of the door on the next vertical piece of molding. "I slid my fingers along it and felt a solid place, while the rest of it felt grooved. I pulled on it and the molding swung open. There's another lever." He pushed the lever down and there was a click.

"The door was already open," observed Jamal.

"I'll go back inside and you close the door from out there," said Dee. "Then see if you can open it. I'll reopen the door if you can't."

Dee stepped inside, Alexi closed the door and they all heard it click into place. They waited a couple of seconds and then Dimitri pulled down on the lever. There was a slight creaking, and the door popped out. Alexi slid his fingers into the opening and pulled the door open. Dee stood there grinning.

"Now we know," said Dee.

Alexi ran his fingers across his forehead. "I still can't believe it." He looked to Dimitri.

"I had no idea. All these years I was just chasing the egg."

Dee had stepped into the hallway. "How will you substantiate or verify the room?" he asked Alexi.

"That's a good question. This is unprecedented. Almost all the Imperial treasures were identified and documented after the revolution or within a few short years. Those that weren't destroyed initially."

"Was there much of that?" asked Jamal.

"The records indicate there was more vandalism than looting. Most of the contents were overwhelming to the original Bolsheviks or revolutionaries. Over the years as the Soviets got established, some of the treasures were relocated to the offices and homes of the party leaders, but they were still documented."

"How will you go about it?" asked Dimitri.

"I suppose I can bring in a gemologist or some sort of expert in amber to examine and maybe try to date the room."

"What about floor plans, architectural renderings?" asked Dee.

"That's a thought. I know there are some available from the last couple hundred years."

"Wouldn't that be public knowledge?" asked Dimitri.

"Not really, no one would have seen them except for the royal family and the Italian architect, Rastrelli. But those are the oldest ones I know of, and they are from the 1830s, after the fire. Catherine had the room moved in 1755."

"Wouldn't the Communists have had access?" asked Jamal.

"Yes, they could have but I don't think any of them ever looked. Once they decided to save the palace, they went about cleaning and restoring but not remodeling in a significant fashion. They just jumped in if they wanted to change something. Then Stalin picked up the idea for the Metro and wanted to continue in the classical Imperial style so they moved on to other projects. They were rather unrestrained."

Dimitri looked at Alexi sharply to which Alexi replied, "You know it's true."

Dimitri nodded. "But it isn't always wise to express your thoughts."

"Wouldn't Rastrelli have worked with some plans, something that preexisted, for his remodeling?" asked Dee.

"I suppose so. And if the plans were thought to be secure, they might reflect the room. I'll check into it. That may be our best hope for authentication."

They were gathered as a group, standing in front of the open door and behind the temporary curtain the workmen had hung for Alexi.

"Well, well, what do we have here?" said a voice that was stepping through the curtain. It was Novak with a Makarov pistol in his hand, a suppressor threaded to the barrel.

The men turned toward him. "Nobody move, hands in the air." He nodded his head toward the open door. "What's in there?"

"King Tut's tomb," said Dee.

Novak turned the pistol toward him. "Fitting place for you to die. Now what's in there?"

No one spoke. Novak waved the pistol at the four men, then at Dee and Jamal. "I knew you two knew something. That's why I had my men follow you from the Winter Palace. At first, we were going to beat it out of you but then we decided to see where you led us. I think that worked out, although I would have preferred beating you."

"We didn't know anything until now," replied Dee.

Novak scoffed and then took over the conversation. "Everyone against the wall, where I can see you, except you." He still had the pistol pointed toward Dee. "Throw him a flashlight." Novak pointed at Alexi.

Alexi pitched it, and Dee caught it.

"Take a step inside, turn the light on and shine it behind you. Try to blind me, I'll shoot you. I may anyway."

Dee did as he was told. Novak took a quick look and then turned to Alexi. "The Amber Room?"

"It could be. We just located it."

"After all these years," Novak said while looking at Dimitri. "The egg and the Amber Room. I'm going to be quite the hero."

"What about the egg?" said Alexi.

Novak looked at him, an amused expression on his face. "I know you have it. My men informed me."

Alexi quickly looked to the others. "I didn't tell anyone."

"You didn't have to, I have eyes everywhere," purred Novak as he turned toward Alexi.

That moment was all Dimitri needed. He pulled his own Makarov, but Novak had seen the motion in his peripheral vision and raised his pistol and fired. There was only a small sound as Dimitri sank to his knees and slumped against the wall.

"It was time. I had grown tired of pursuing him," said Novak to the remaining group.

"What's going on here," said a booming voice as an older man and a striking middle-aged woman stepped through the curtain.

Novak whirled toward them and didn't notice Dimitri sliding his arm up and steadying himself against the wall. Dimitri pointed his pistol and fired two rounds into the back of

Novak's head, which literally exploded across the wall behind him. Dimitri slumped and slid back down the wall.

The older man turned toward Alexi and bellowed again, "What's going on here?"

The woman had gone to stand beside Alexi.

Jamal turned to Dee. "Mrs. Alexi?"

"Who knows, let's check on Dimitri."

They scurried across and Dee felt his neck for a pulse. Looking up at Jamal, Dee shook his head.

"Dimitri was one of the good guys," replied Jamal.

"Yeah. "

"He saved our lives."

"Several times."

———

ALEXI WAS POINTING TOWARD DIMITRI, DEE, AND JAMAL.

"Dimitri found the missing Fabergé pearl egg. It led us to this room. The original amber room. There was a message in the egg."

"Amazing discovery," said the older man.

Dee and Jamal had risen and approached the men.

Alexi looked at them. "This is Marat Sokolov, the Minister of Culture, and this is my wife, Maria. This is Dee Sanders and Jamal Jones, they were working with Dimitri."

The minister nodded.

Alexi continued. "Novak pulled a gun. Dimitri was defending us."

The minister pointed at the two downed men. "Yes, Dimitri Kuznetsov will not be missed, and Novak Novachek, he was inconsequential. But this discovery, this is of great consequence. This is everything. Come and show me this discovery that you and I have made." They stepped into the room and disappeared.

Dee and Jamal stood silently for a moment. The woman stood opposite them. They looked at her for the first time. She was dark-haired and dark-eyed. Her hair and her legs were long. She had a striking figure, and a delicately beautiful face, like a porcelain doll.

She held out her hand. "I'm Maria, Alexi's wife."

"Dee Sanders."

"Jamal Jones."

They all shook hands.

"Could you tell us how you happened to be here?" asked Dee. "We're happy you were. It was lucky for us."

She smiled. "Alexi texted me yesterday and said that Dimitri had discovered a room in the palace and that it might be of extreme historical and monetary value. Also that he was being threatened by Novak Novachek and could I help. I contacted Marat and advised him of the finding. He insisted we come and see. We just happened in, apparently as things were developing."

"We're grateful," said Jamal.

"Did you know Dimitri?" asked Dee.

She glanced over at his body. "Yes. He and Alexi and I knew each other when we were younger, and we spent a lot of time together. It's been a number of years since I last saw him."

She paused for a moment as if reflecting on their past. "We were in school together. They were already friends. I was a special student, segregated from the others. I was well-educated, spoke several languages, and was on my way to a career as a dancer when I met them. Unfortunately, I grew too tall and had to return to being a regular student. When I chose Alexi, it broke Dimitri's heart. But then I was selected to tutor. One of the party's top political officials had been a fan of my dancing and had a daughter who wanted to learn. Then I began to tutor other subjects, languages and art. Then another political minister took an interest in me."

"Is that considered an honor?" asked Dee.

"Yes, and no. If I'd been single, it would have been easier, but you don't say no to a high-ranking party member. He was older and not very demanding. I thought it would pass. But instead, he wasn't very possessive and began to share me with his friends, the other ministers."

Dee and Jamal heard the sadness in her voice and saw her face lengthen.

She continued. "Soon it was a group of two or three, often six nights or days a week. I tutored less and saw Alexi infrequently. It's a road that once you start down, there's no way back. But, those contacts, that intimacy, is what enabled me to help Alexi."

"And what saved us," added Jamal.

She smiled. "Each day I grow older. Some morning I know I will wake up and be replaced. Will I resume tutoring, return to Alexi, if he'll have me, or be removed or eliminated for hearing some carelessly whispered detail that I care nothing about, but they do?"

ALEXI AND THE MINISTER EMERGED FROM THE ROOM. THE minister was animated in his gestures, his face highlighted with excitement. He took Maria by the arm and led her back into the hallway.

Alexi stepped across to Dee and Jamal. "The minister is ecstatic. He plans to take credit for the discoveries with a nod to me for assistance."

Dee and Jamal looked at him with blank faces.

"That's how it works here. I'm just grateful to be included at all. I should probably thank my wife for that."

"He can do that?" asked Jamal.

"Absolutely."

"Can we do anything for you or about the situation?" asked Dee.

"Yes, accept his thanks and let me put you on a plane to wherever you want to go, soon."

"He wants us out of here?" asked Jamal.

"Yes."

"How about two first-class tickets to the Maldives?" asked Dee.

"On it," replied Alexi, who then turned and led them toward his office.

Following along behind, Jamal whispered to Dee, "I guess there's no reward?"

"Actually there is, we found the treasure, and we escaped with our lives."

EPILOGUE

Here I lie on the cold, cold ground. I look back at my spaniel, Jemmy. He lies silent and still, there are snakes no more. Soon I will join him and we will be together again, forever.

My name is Anastasia. I am the last Romanoff, the final nail in the coffin of Imperial Russia. I saved the pearl, and I eluded my captors and lived for five days.

ENJOY THIS BOOK?

A note from Author LP Snyder

If you've enjoyed this book, I would be very grateful if you could spend just five minutes leaving a review (it can be as short as you like) on the book's Amazon page and on Goodreads or BookBub.

Thank you very much.

ACKNOWLEDGMENTS

From Author L.P. Snyder

Thank you to all the readers who have made these books successful. That has encouraged me to continue and here we are. I hope you enjoy reading the books as much as I enjoy writing them.

I want to thank Vince Conti for the beautiful cover, Elizabeth Mackey for the cover consultation, and Jamie Lee Scott for the amazing travel map. I especially want to thank my editor, Lisa Lee who helped me pull this book together from a concept to a finished product. Also, thanks are in order to my fellow authors Kelly Utt and Shannon Brown for their insight and support, and finally to my wife Diana.

ABOUT THE AUTHOR

LP Snyder is a life-long reader who, at the last minute, decided to become a writer. It's been a great experience, and he wonders why it took so long to decide! Having read a little of most genres, LP decided to stick with his favorites—adventure, espionage, and crime thrillers! If you like fast-paced, humorous, action-filled, suspense thrillers, he's your Huckleberry!

Newsletter subscribers receive bonus content, including short stories and extended epilogues. Don't be afraid to ride that wave!

Sign up at www.lpsnyder.com.